Dear Reader, let's fasten our belts and start our galactic journey. Together, we will make our discovery.

Harmony's Odyssey

Harmony's Odyssey: Earth's Journey Through Shadow and Light

Author

Dokali Megharief

Preface

In the vast expanse of the cosmos, where stars twinkle like scattered diamonds and galaxies swirl in majestic patterns, the fate of a single planet may seem inconsequential. Yet, in this tale, Earth's destiny becomes the focal point of an interstellar coalition's concern. As we embark on this journey through "Harmony's Odyssey," we prepare to witness a story transcending the boundaries of time, space, and species.

Earth, celebrated for its unparalleled biodiversity and vibrant ecosystems, has reached a critical juncture. The relentless pursuit of technological advancement and unchecked exploitation of natural resources have driven the planet to the brink. What was once a haven of life and beauty now struggles under the weight of pollution, climate change, and ecological imbalance.

The United Galaxies Council (UGC), a distinguished assembly of advanced civilizations, has taken notice. From their vantage points across the Milky Way, they have observed the ripple effects of Earth's actions, which extend far beyond its atmosphere. The council's decision to convene on Marsland, a neutral territory renowned for its red forests and crystalline cities, marks the beginning of an unprecedented intervention.

As you delve into the pages of this narrative, you will encounter a myriad of characters, each representing their unique worlds and perspectives. The council members, from the energy beings of Andromeda to the aquatic Zephyrians, bring their collective wisdom and technological prowess to the table. Their discussions, debates, and decisions will shape the future of Earth and its place within the cosmic community.

This story is not just a chronicle of intergalactic diplomacy and environmental restoration; it is a reflection of our own choices and their far-reaching consequences. It urges us to consider nature's delicate balance, the importance of sustainable progress, and the interconnectedness of all life forms.

"Earth's Journey Through Shadow and Light" is a testament to hope, resilience, and the possibility of redemption. It invites you to ponder existence's profound questions of existence and envision a future where harmony prevails. As the UGC delegates navigate the complexities of intervention, they remind us that even in the darkest times, there is a path toward light.

Welcome to a story that bridges worlds, unites species, and challenges us to rethink our role in the universe. May it inspire you to seek solutions, embrace diversity, and cherish the planet we call home.

Dokali Megharief

INTRODUCTION

In the year 2424, the United Galaxies Council (UGC), a coalition of advanced civilizations from across the Milky Way, gathered for an unprecedented assembly on Marsland. This neutral territory, celebrated for its vibrant red forests that stretched like a painter's brush across the landscape and cities that sparkled with crystalline structures reflecting the light of two suns, served as the perfect backdrop for discussions of cosmic importance.

The council members, representing a myriad of species and planets, arrived in their sleek StarCraft, each one a testament to the technological marvels of their respective worlds. The air buzzed with a multitude of languages, some spoken and others transmitted telepathically, as delegates prepared for the session.

The sole item on the agenda was a matter of grave concern that had rippled through the space-time continuum: the environmental impact of Earth's inhabitants. The blue planet, once a jewel of biodiversity, had seen its natural resources depleted at an alarming rate. The Earthlings' relentless pursuit of progress had not only scared their home planet but also left a trail of debris and disruption in the cosmic expanse.

The UGC had long observed Earth from a distance, noting the rise in temperatures, the melting of polar ice caps, and the alarming rate of species extinction. But now, the effects were being felt beyond Earth's atmosphere. Space expeditions had left a graveyard of satellites and spacecraft orbiting the planet, and interstellar travel had introduced invasive species to fragile ecosystems on other worlds.

The council was tasked with deliberating potential interventions. Could they introduce advanced technologies to reverse the damage? Should they impose strict regulations on space travel and resource extraction? Or was it time for a more direct approach, one that would involve contacting Earth directly to offer guidance and support?

As the delegates took their seats in the grand hall, a structure carved from the native red stone and enclosed in a dome of transparent diamond, the weight of their decision loomed over them. The future of Earth and its role in the United Galaxies depended on the outcome of this extraordinary session. It seemed that one planet's fate had become the concern of an entire galaxy.

Chapter 1: The Gathering Storm

As the delegates arrived, their ships descended through Marsland's scarlet canopies, casting prismatic shadows on the ground below.
The representatives of various star systems, each with their own unique forms and philosophies, shared a common worry: Earth's reckless disposal of waste was reaching a critical point.

The council chamber, a grand amphitheater carved from a single Martian mega crystal, buzzed with tension. At the center stood the UGC President, Xylo-Thorax of Andromeda, a being of pure energy contained within a shimmering exoskeleton.

"Esteemed members of the UGC," Xylo-Thorax began, "we are here to address the 'Earthy' dilemma. Their planet, once a gem in our galaxy's crown, now suffocates under layers of pollution. Worse still, their space debris endangers all interstellar travel. We must act for the sake of our shared future."

The chamber fell silent as the gravity of the situation sank in. The delegates, beings of various shapes and sizes, from the aquatic Zephyrians to the crystalline entities of Crystallon exchanged glances, their expressions ranging from concern to outright fear.

Xylo-Thorax continued, "The Earthlings, in their pursuit of progress, have forgotten the ancient laws of cosmic balance. Their machines belch out toxins that poison the air and waters, not just of their world but of the cosmos. We've observed the dying of stars, the mutation of intergalactic flora, and the disruption of the astral currents."

A murmur rippled through the assembly as Xylo-Thorax displayed holographic images of Earth's oceans, choked with plastic, and its skies, veiled in smog. "This," he declared, "is the result of one species' negligence. And not just their natural environment suffers—diseases of their making plague their own kind."

A delegate from Sirius, a luminous figure with eyes like twin suns, rose to speak. "We have extended our hand in friendship to Earth before, offering them technology to cleanse their world. Yet they have turned away, blinded by greed and short-sighted politics."

The Martian representative, a towering figure with skin like red rock, added, "Their refusal to join the Galactic Accord on Waste Management is a slap in the face to all civilizations that have worked to maintain the delicate balance of the cosmos."

The room erupted into a heated debate, with suggestions ranging from imposing sanctions on Earth to launching a full-scale intervention. But amidst the cacophony, a small voice spoke up—a young delegate from a recently inducted planet, Terra Nova.

"May I propose an alternative?" the Terra Novan asked, her voice steady despite the eyes now fixed upon her. "Earth is a world of immense diversity and potential. They are young and have much to learn, but they are also capable of great change. Instead of coercion, why not offer guidance? Perhaps a coalition of mentors to help them see the error of their ways and heal their world together."

The chamber quieted as the delegates considered this new approach. Xylo-Thorax nodded thoughtfully. "A wise suggestion from one of our youngest members. It is decided then. We shall form a delegation of the willing to go to Earth, not as conquerors, but as teachers and healers."

The meeting adjourned with a sense of cautious optimism. The storm was still gathering, but now there was a glimmer of hope that together, they could weather it and restore balance to the galaxy.

Chapter 2: Earth's Echo

The Earth's delegate, Dr. Luna Marez, stepped forward. Her holographic form flickered with urgency. "I come bearing Earth's plea and promise. We've awakened to our errors and are striving to mend our ways. Our new initiative, 'Terra Firma,' aims to cleanse our oceans and skies, and 'Stellar Custodians' will clear the orbital paths."

Whispers of skepticism rippled through the assembly. The Zephyrians from the Horsehead Nebula scoffed at the notion, their gaseous forms undulating with doubt. "Promises are as fleeting as comets," they hissed. "We demand action, not words." Dr. Marez nodded, understanding the assembly's concerns. "Actions indeed," she agreed. "Terra Firma has already deployed fleets of drones to the Pacific Gyre, where they are extracting tons of plastic daily. Our skies, once gray with the smog of industry, now see the return of birds as emissions controls and green technologies take root."

The assembly watched as Dr. Marez presented real-time feeds of Earth's recovery efforts. The drones, like a swarm of bees, worked in unison while cities below thrived with new greenery.

A Crystallon delegate, their body a lattice of living minerals, spoke up. "Your efforts are commendable, but what of the Stellar Custodians? The debris field around your planet is a hazard to all."

Dr. Marez gestured, and the hologram shifted to show the Custodians at work. With their magnetic nets, these robotic shepherds were corralling defunct satellites and spent rocket stages, guiding them toward incineration in the atmosphere.

"The Stellar Custodians are not just cleaners but also guardians," Dr. Marez explained. "They serve as a symbol of our commitment to safeguarding the pathways we all share among the stars."

The Terra Novan delegate from Chapter 1, now a vocal supporter of Earth, chimed in. "Let us not forget that every civilization has its dawn. Earth is at the cusp of theirs, and they are learning, as we all did, the balance between progress and preservation."

The debate shifted from criticism to collaboration. The assembly discussed forming a 'Galactic Green Alliance,' pooling knowledge and resources to tackle Earth's issues and environmental challenges across the galaxy.

As the session drew to a close, Dr. Marez's hologram shimmered with hope. "Together, we can turn the tide against the damage done. Earth is ready to join hands with all of you for a cleaner, brighter future."

This chapter ends with the delegates agreeing to reconvene and Earth presenting a detailed report on their progress. The storm had not yet passed, but Earth's echo resonated throughout the galaxy, signaling a new era of interstellar stewardship.

Chapter 3: The Fractured Accord

A troubling report surfaced as the United Galaxies Council (UGC) drafted the Galactic Environmental Accord. Intelligence from covert surveillance drones revealed that Earth's commitment to the 'Terra Firma' initiative was wavering. Industrial magnates and political leaders, driven by greed and short-term gains, were secretly flouting the waste management protocols.

Once filled with cautious optimism, the UGC's chamber now echoed with outrage and disappointment. Xylo-Thorax's exoskeleton pulsed with a dim light, reflecting the somber mood. "We face a dire choice," he declared. "If Earth cannot honor its pledge, we must consider more drastic measures."

The Zephyrians, still skeptical from the start, proposed a motion: "Should Earth fail to comply, we authorize the creation of the 'Galactic Guardians.' These enforcers will have the power to impose sanctions, quarantine the planet, and take control of Earth's waste management by force if necessary."

Dr. Luna Marez pleaded for patience, "Give us time; many on Earth are true to their word and are fighting for change. We need support, not threats."

But the motion passed. The UGC would not risk the safety of the cosmos for the sake of one planet's internal strife. The Galactic Guardians were to be assembled—a fleet of formidable ships equipped with technology capable of disabling polluting facilities and capturing rogue waste.

The news of the Guardians' impending arrival sent shockwaves through Earth's societies. Protests erupted in cities worldwide, with citizens demanding accountability from their leaders. The Terra Firma initiative, once a beacon of hope, now stood as a testament to broken promises.

In the UGC, a faction of pacifists led by the empathetic beings of Elysium voiced their dissent. "We must not meet secrecy with aggression," they urged. "The Guardians could incite a war with Earth that could spread across planets and star systems."

Xylo-Thorax, though firm in his stance, acknowledged the pacifists' concerns. "The Guardians will act only as a last resort. Our primary goal remains diplomacy and education. Earth must understand the consequences of their actions, not just for their world, but for the entire galaxy."

Back on Earth, Dr. Marez worked tirelessly to rally the forces of change. She formed alliances with environmental groups, innovators, and even some forward-thinking industrialists. Together, they launched a counter-initiative, 'Project Blue Dawn,' aimed at revitalizing the Terra Firma goals and proving Earth's sincerity to the UGC.

As the chapter closes, Earth's fate hangs in the balance. The Galactic Guardians stand ready to intervene while Earth's champions of change strive to avert a crisis. The fractured accord has revealed interstellar politics' complexities and trust's fragile nature.

Chapter 4: Earth's Ultimatum

The UGC issued an ultimatum to Earth: adhere to the Accord or face the Guardians. Earth's leaders, faced with the reality of losing their autonomy, convened an emergency summit. The threat of the Guardians united factions like never before, and a global movement emerged, demanding compliance with the UGC's mandates.

The 'Terra Firma' and 'Stellar Custodians' initiatives were revitalized with new vigor, and the people of Earth worked alongside the UGC's envoys to restore their planet and its celestial surroundings.

In the end, the presence of the Galactic Guardians was not needed. Earth had heeded the warning and took its place as a responsible member of the interstellar community. The UGC's firm stance had steered Earth back from the brink, ensuring a cleaner future for all.

The emergency summit was a whirlwind of activity. Leaders from every nation gathered, their faces etched with concern and determination. They debated, negotiated, and finally united under a common cause: the survival of their home planet.

The Guardians, a fleet of ships stationed just beyond the Moon's orbit, stood as a silent testament to the UGC's resolve. Their sleek forms, bristling with advanced technology, reminded us of what could be lost—or gained.

On Earth, the Terra Firma initiative took on a new life. Engineers, scientists, and volunteers from around the world collaborated on projects that spanned from the depths of the oceans to the edges of the atmosphere. The once-abandoned clean-up operations were now beacons of progress, with advancements in bioremediation and nanotechnology leading the charge.

The Stellar Custodians, too, saw a resurgence in support. Astronauts and robots worked in tandem to clear the cluttered orbits while new regulations were put in place on the ground to prevent future space debris.

As the deadline approached, the UGC watched closely. Xylo-Thorax, who had been a stern figure throughout the crisis, now showed signs of approval. "Earth has shown a remarkable capacity for change," he observed. "Perhaps there is hope for this young species yet."

The global movement that had started as a cry for survival evolved into a powerful force for change. 'Earth United' became the rallying cry as humanity recognized their planet's value and place in the cosmos.

The Guardians never descended upon Earth. Instead, they became a symbol of what could be achieved when the threat of destruction was met with unity and action.

As the chapter concludes, Earth's leaders sign the Accord with the UGC, cementing their commitment to a sustainable future. Once harbingers of doom, the Guardians now serve as protectors of a planet reborn, and the UGC hails Earth as a model of environmental redemption.

Chapter 5: The Galactic Standoff

The United Galaxies Council's (UGC) patience had worn thin. Earth's defiance had escalated to a point where diplomatic solutions were no longer viable. Once a peaceful assembly, the UGC was now on the brink of enforcing its most severe sanctions.

Xylo-Thorax addressed the council with a stern tone that resonated through the chamber, "The time for warnings has passed. Earth's leaders have ignored our ultimatums, and their actions now threaten the very fabric of our interstellar society. We must deploy the Galactic Guardians."

The council members, though heavy-hearted, agreed. A fleet of the most advanced Guardian ships was dispatched to Earth's orbit. Their orders were clear: disable any and all polluting industries and secure the space lanes from hazardous debris.

The Guardians, a symbol of the UGC's might, were not just enforcers but also harbingers of change. As they positioned themselves around Earth, their presence was a final, stark reminder to humanity of the consequences of their negligence.

On Earth, the news of the Guardians' arrival sparked a global epiphany. The threat of intervention galvanized the people into action like never before. In a remarkable display of unity, governments, corporations, and citizens came together to address the crisis head-on.

The world witnessed an unprecedented wave of innovation and cooperation. New treaties were signed, and old rivalries were set aside in the face of a common enemy: their own past actions. The 'Green Revolution, as it came to be known, saw the rapid deployment of sustainable technologies and the dismantling of the most harmful industries.

As the deadline loomed, the Guardians observed the transformation taking place below. Their sensors, capable of detecting even the smallest pollution particle, recorded a significant decrease in contaminants. The once murky atmosphere began to clear, revealing the blue of oceans and the green of forests.

Xylo-Thorax, monitoring the situation from the UGC headquarters, felt a glimmer of hope. "Perhaps we were wrong to doubt them," he mused. "Earthlings have shown a capacity for resilience and adaptability that is truly remarkable."

The council convened once more, this time to discuss the Guardians' withdrawal. The debate was intense, but in the end, they decided to give Earth a chance to continue its redemption path without the Guardians' looming threat.

The fleet received the order to stand down and return to their stations across the galaxy. As they departed, they left behind a legacy that would be remembered for generations. Earth had been on the precipice of disaster, but when faced with the ultimate test, it had risen to the challenge.

The chapter closes with Earth's leaders addressing the UGC, expressing their gratitude and reaffirming their commitment to the Galactic Environmental Accord. The standoff had ended, not with conflict, but with a newfound determination to safeguard their home and contribute to the well-being of the interstellar community.

Chapter 6: Earth's Rebellion

News of the approaching fleet sparked a rebellion on Earth. The people, feeling betrayed by their leaders' greed and the UGC's heavy-handed tactics, rallied under a new banner, 'Terra's Shield.' They vowed to protect their sovereignty at all costs.

Dr. Luna Marez, once a voice of reason, now became a symbol of resistance. "We will not bow to the tyranny of the stars," she proclaimed. "Earth stands united, and we will fight for our right to self-determination."

News of the approaching fleet sparked a rebellion on Earth. The people, feeling betrayed by their leaders' greed and the UGC's heavy-handed tactics, rallied under a new banner, 'Terra's Shield.' They vowed to protect their sovereignty at all costs.

Dr. Luna Marez, once a voice of reason, now became a symbol of resistance. "We will not bow to the tyranny of the stars," she proclaimed. "Earth stands united, and we will fight for our right to self-determination."

The rebellion, fueled by a mix of fear and defiance, spread like wildfire. From the sprawling megacities to the smallest rural communities, humans of all walks of life joined the cause. Terra's Shield became more than a movement; it was a declaration of Earth's indomitable spirit.

Underground networks formed, connecting scientists, engineers, and strategists. They worked in secret, developing countermeasures against the Guardians' technology. Hackers infiltrated the UGC's communication channels, seeking to delay the fleet's advance or turn their systems against them.

Dr. Marez, leading the charge, called upon Earth's greatest minds to devise a plan. "We must show the UGC that Earth is not a rogue planet to be disciplined, but a sovereign world capable of governing itself," she urged.

The resistance's efforts were not in vain. As the Guardians drew closer, they found Earth's defenses far more formidable than anticipated. Shields of electromagnetic energy repelled their scanning beams, and drones swarmed the Guardians' ships, hindering their progress.

The UGC, observing the situation, was taken aback by the resilience shown by Earth. Xylo-Thorax, who had never witnessed such fierce determination in a species, began to question the council's decision. "Have we pushed them too far?" he pondered.

Meanwhile, on Earth, the movement gave rise to a new era of unity. Political boundaries dissolved as humanity realized that their true enemy was not the stars but their own divisive past. The rebellion brought about an unprecedented level of cooperation, sparking a renaissance of culture, science, and philosophy.

As the deadline for the ultimatum approached, Earth presented a united front. The Guardians, now hovering in orbit, faced a planet armored not just with technology, but with the collective will of its people.

In a historic broadcast, Dr. Marez addressed both Earth and the UGC. "We stand at a crossroads," she declared. "The path we choose today will define the future of not just our world, but of the interstellar community. We ask the UGC to stand down and recognize our sovereignty. In return, we pledge to uphold the principles of the Galactic Environmental Accord, not under duress, but as free citizens of the galaxy."

The chapter concludes with the UGC deliberating. The rebellion had shown that Earth was not a planet to be tamed but a force to be reckoned with. The outcome of their decision remained uncertain, but one thing was clear: Earth would never be the same again.

Chapter 7: The Siege of Earth

The Guardian fleet arrived to find a planet armored for war. Earth's orbital defenses, a network of satellites and space stations, unleashed a barrage of energy against the Guardians. The battle was fierce, lighting up the sky as a warning to all who watched from afar.

The UGC watched in horror as the conflict they had sought to prevent unfolded. Xylo-Thorax, realizing the gravity of the situation, called for an immediate ceasefire. "This is not the way," he declared. "We must find peace, or we risk losing Earth and ourselves to the void."

The siege of Earth was not just a physical confrontation but a clash of ideologies. The Guardians, once seen as protectors, were now viewed as invaders. Earth's defenses, powered by the collective will of its people, stood firm against the advanced alien technology.

As the battle raged on, a small group of Earth's diplomats and UGC mediators gathered in secret, desperate to find a diplomatic solution. They knew that the longer the conflict continued, the greater the chance of irreversible damage to both sides.

The mediators proposed a bold plan: a summit on the Moon, neutral ground where leaders from Earth and the UGC could negotiate without the threat of immediate violence. The proposal was risky, but with each passing moment, the stakes grew higher.

Xylo-Thorax, his exoskeleton now pulsing with a soft light of conciliation, agreed to the summit. "Let us meet and discuss our futures," he said. "The cosmos is vast enough for all of us to coexist peacefully."

The summit on the Moon was a historic event. Delegates from Earth and representatives of the UGC sat across from each other, the Earth hanging in the sky behind them—a poignant reminder of what was at risk.

The negotiations were tense, with both sides presenting their grievances and demands. Earth's leaders argued for autonomy and respect for their sovereignty, while the UGC insisted on strict adherence to environmental regulations to protect the galaxy.

As hours turned into days, a breakthrough finally came. A young delegate from Earth, a scientist who had dedicated her life to sustainable living, presented a new vision for Earth's future. "We can be the model of environmental recovery," she said. "Not just for ourselves, but for all civilizations that may one day face the same challenges."

Moved by her passion and the tangible plans she presented, the UGC delegates began to see Earth not as a rogue planet but as a potential beacon of hope.

The siege ended not with the might of weapons but with the power of words and promises. The UGC agreed to lift the blockade, and Earth pledged to lead by example, transforming its industries and societies to be sustainable and environmentally conscious.

The chapter concludes with dismantling Earth's orbital defenses and the departure of the Guardian fleet. The skies above were clear once more, not just of ships and weapons but of the fear and uncertainty that had gripped the planet.

The Siege of Earth would be remembered not as a battle but as the turning point when Earth and the UGC learned that the path to harmony lay not in dominance but in understanding and cooperation.

Chapter 8: The Path to Peace

The siege lasted days, with neither side yielding. But amidst the chaos, a silent movement grew. Scientists and environmentalists from Earth and emissaries from the UGC met in secret, forging a new plan to end the conflict and heal the planet.

They presented their solution to both sides: a joint Earth-UGC initiative that would not only clean up Earth and its surroundings but also empower its people to maintain their environment without external enforcement.

Moved by the prospect of peace, both Earth and the UGC agreed. The Guardians withdrew, and 'Terra's Shield' stood down. The planet was battered, but its spirit was unbroken. Together, Earth and the UGC embarked on a new journey, one of cooperation and mutual respect.

The initiative, dubbed 'Project Harmonia,' was ambitious. It aimed to integrate advanced UGC technologies with Earth's own efforts to rehabilitate its ecosystems. The project was divided into several key areas: atmospheric purification, oceanic restoration, terrestrial rebalancing, and space debris management.

Atmospheric purification stations, towering structures reaching high into the sky, were constructed around the globe. These stations worked tirelessly to filter pollutants from the air, restoring the atmosphere to its pre-industrial clarity.

Fleets of drones patrolled the oceans, collecting waste and repairing the damage done to marine habitats. Coral reefs began to flourish once again, and species on the brink of extinction found new hope for survival.

On land, vast reforestation campaigns were launched. Deserts bloomed as innovative irrigation techniques were employed, and urban areas were transformed into green havens, with rooftop gardens and vertical farms becoming the norm.

Above Earth, the space debris that had long been a blight on the planet's orbit was methodically cleared. The UGC provided technology that made the process efficient and safe, ensuring that the pathways through the stars were open and secure for all.

As the project progressed, Earth's society underwent a transformation. The economy shifted towards sustainability, with green jobs replacing those in polluting industries. Education systems were reformed to emphasize environmental stewardship and interstellar diplomacy.

The Guardians, once feared enforcers, now served as advisors and allies. They shared their knowledge freely, helping to guide humanity on its path to becoming a truly galactic civilization.

Dr. Luna Marez, the symbol of Earth's rebellion, became the ambassador to the UGC. Her voice, once raised in defiance, now spoke of unity and shared goals. "We have learned much from our past," she said in a landmark address to the council. "But it is our future that now unites us."

The chapter concludes with the inauguration of the first joint Earth-UGC environmental summit, held on the newly rejuvenated Earth. The event celebrated what had been achieved and pledged to continue the work that lay ahead.

The Path to Peace was not just a chapter in a book; it was a new chapter in the history of Earth and the UGC—a testament to the power of cooperation and the enduring spirit of a planet that refused to give up.

Chapter 9: The Reconciliation

In the aftermath of the siege, Earth and the United Galaxies Council (UGC) faced the daunting task of rebuilding trust. The scars of battle served as a stark reminder of the perils of miscommunication and the cost of war.

The UGC, led by Xylo-Thorax, extended an olive branch to Earth. "Let us not be defined by our conflicts but by our capacity to overcome them," he urged. The council proposed the 'Intergalactic Restoration Initiative' (IRI), a comprehensive plan to repair the damage done to Earth's environment and infrastructure.

The IRI was a multi-phased project that aimed to address the immediate needs of Earth's recovery while laying the groundwork for long-term sustainability.

The first phase involved deploying medical and engineering teams to the most affected areas, providing aid, and beginning the reconstruction process

Xylo-Thorax personally oversaw the delivery of advanced medical technology to Earth's hospitals, where it was used to treat those injured during the conflict. The technology not only healed physical wounds but also helped to alleviate the psychological trauma suffered by many.

Engineering squads, composed of experts from various UGC member planets, worked alongside Earth's own engineers. They shared knowledge and resources, repairing infrastructure and ensuring that new constructions were environmentally friendly and resilient.

The second phase of the IRI focused on ecological restoration. Teams of biologists and ecologists from Earth and the UGC collaborated to revitalize damaged ecosystems. They reintroduced native species, cleaned polluted waterways, and implemented advanced soil regeneration techniques.

One of the most ambitious projects was the 'Great Green Wall, a planetary effort to plant a belt of trees across Earth's deserts. This initiative not only combated desertification but also created jobs and strengthened communities.

The third phase was dedicated to education and cultural exchange. The UGC established interstellar exchange programs, inviting Earth's students and professionals to learn from the advanced societies of the galaxy. In return, Earth shared its rich cultural heritage, and the lessons learned from its environmental challenges.

As the IRI progressed, Earth began to transform. Cities became greener, the air became cleaner, and the oceans teemed with life once more. The initiative had not only repaired the damage but also brought about a renaissance of innovation and cooperation.

Xylo-Thorax, addressing the UGC assembly, reflected on the journey. "The Reconciliation has shown us that unity is not just a lofty ideal, but a practical path to a brighter future," he said. "Together, Earth and the UGC have turned the tide of despair into a wave of hope."

The chapter concludes with the celebration of the first 'Day of Reconciliation,' a new galactic holiday commemorating the peace forged between Earth and the UGC. It was a day of joy, reflection, and a renewed commitment to a united galaxy.

Chapter 10: Terra's Renaissance

Earth embraced the IRI with open arms. The initiative was more than just a repair program; it was a catalyst for innovation. New technologies emerged, harnessing renewable energy and promoting sustainability. Earth's cities flourished once again, becoming beacons of green technology and ecological harmony.

The 'Terra's Shield' rebels, now champions of peace, worked alongside UGC engineers. Together, they developed a network of satellites, The Green Canopy, which monitored environmental health and provided real-time data to ensure compliance with the IRI.

Earth's renaissance was marked by a surge in creativity and technological advancement. The Green Canopy became the planet's guardian, its eyes in the sky keeping a vigilant watch over its health. It was a symbol of Earth's commitment to the future—a future where technology and nature existed in harmony.

In the cities, urban landscapes transformed. Rooftops sprouted gardens, and vertical farms climbed towards the sky. Public transportation systems were overhauled, now powered by clean energy and designed to minimize congestion and pollution.

Education systems worldwide were reformed to include environmental science, sustainability, and space studies curricula. Children learned not only about their own planet but also about the wider galaxy and Earth's place within it.

The arts flourished in this new era, with artists drawing inspiration from Earth's revival. Music, literature, and visual arts reflected the optimism of the times, and cultural festivals celebrated the unity between Earth and the UGC.

Economically, the shift to green industries created a boom in jobs and opportunities. Innovators and entrepreneurs thrived, launching startups that turned waste into resources and pollution into energy.

The former rebels of Terra's Shield redirected their passion towards advocacy and education. They organized community projects and workshops, teaching people how to live more sustainably and reduce their ecological footprint.

Impressed by Earth's turnaround, the UGC used it as a case study for other worlds facing environmental challenges. Delegations from across the galaxy visited Earth to learn from its experiences and take back knowledge to their home planets.

As the IRI's projects reached completion, Earth held a grand ceremony to celebrate its transformation. The event was broadcast throughout the galaxy, showcasing the planet's lush landscapes, clean waters, and clear skies.

Dr. Luna Marez, once a voice of resistance, now stood before the assembly as a leader of progress. "We have shown that from the ashes of conflict can rise a phoenix of innovation and unity," she declared. "Let Terra's Renaissance be a beacon of hope for all civilizations that aspire to live in harmony with their environment."

The chapter concludes with the inauguration of the Terra Institute of Galactic Studies, a center of learning and research dedicated to fostering interstellar relations and environmental stewardship. Earth has not only healed itself but also become a leader in the galactic community, guiding others on the path to peace and sustainability.

Chapter 11: The Cosmic Symposium

To celebrate the IRI's success, the UGC hosted the first 'Cosmic Symposium' on Marsland. Delegates from across the galaxies gathered to share knowledge and discuss the future of interstellar environmental policy.

Dr. Luna Marez, representing Earth, delivered a moving speech. "From the ashes of discord, we have risen united. Let this symposium be a testament to what we can achieve when we choose collaboration over conflict."

The symposium was a grand affair held in the Crystal Halls of Marsland, a location chosen for its neutral standing and breathtaking beauty. The halls, with their translucent walls and ceilings, allowed the attendees to gaze upon the Martian landscape and the cosmos beyond, serving as a constant reminder of the universe they all shared.

The agenda was packed with workshops, panels, and roundtable discussions. Topics ranged from the technical, such as terraforming and climate control—to the philosophical, including the ethics of planetary stewardship and the role of sentient beings in the cosmos.

One of the highlights was a panel featuring the engineers of 'The Green Canopy.' They discussed the challenges and triumphs of creating the satellite network that now protected Earth. The panel ended with a live demonstration, showing real-time data and the

Canopy's positive impact on Earth's recovery.

Dr. Marez's speech was a focal point of the symposium. She spoke of Earth's journey from the brink of ecological collapse to a world reborn. "We have learned that our planet is not just a home but a responsibility," she said. "The IRI was the beginning, but the work continues. We must remain vigilant and dedicated to preserving the delicate balance of our ecosystems."

The symposium also served as a cultural exchange. Earth's delegates brought with them music, art, and cuisine, sharing their planet's rich heritage with the galaxy. In return, they experienced the diverse cultures of the UGC, each with its own unique contributions to the tapestry of galactic society.

A key outcome of the symposium was the 'Marsland Declaration,' a document outlining the shared commitment of all present to uphold and advance the principles of the IRI. It called for ongoing cooperation, sharing knowledge and resources, and establishing a permanent interstellar environmental task force.

As the symposium drew to a close, a ceremony was held under the stars. Delegates from each world placed a fragment of their home soil into a common garden, symbolizing their united front in the face of environmental challenges.

The chapter concludes with Dr. Marez looking out over the garden, now a mosaic of soils from countless worlds. "This garden," she mused, "is a microcosm of our universe, diverse, beautiful, and interdependent. May it thrive, just as our alliance shall, for eons to come."

Chapter 12: The Legacy of Marsland

The signing of the Marsland Accord was a momentous occasion that would be remembered throughout the ages. The United Planetary Fund (UPF), established under the Accord, was a beacon of hope for planets struggling with environmental challenges, symbolizing the UGC's commitment to aiding those in need.

The UPF was not merely a repository of funds; it was a hub of innovation and collaboration. It financed projects that ranged from atmospheric purification to wildlife conservation and from waste management to renewable energy development. The Fund also facilitated the exchange of knowledge and technology between advanced and developing planetary systems, ensuring that no world was left behind.

The Marsland Accord itself was a comprehensive treaty that addressed a multitude of environmental issues. It set forth guidelines for sustainable development, conservation efforts, and the responsible use of natural resources. It also established a framework for responding to ecological disasters, with rapid deployment teams ready to assist at a moment's notice.

The Accord's legacy is evident in the thriving ecosystems of once-barren planets, the clear skies of industrial worlds that have turned away from fossil fuels, and the vibrant biodiversity that has been preserved for future generations.

Epilogue: A New Era (Expanded)

The legacy of the events that transpired on Earth and Marsland was passed down through generations. The UGC, once a symbol of authority, had become a symbol of unity and hope. The Green Canopy satellites, ever-watchful, served as a constant reminder of the delicate balance between progress and preservation.

The New Era was characterized by a galactic community that valued life's sanctity and the planets' health. The UGC's role had evolved from enforcer to mentor, guiding civilizations towards harmonious living with their environments.

Education systems across the galaxy now included the history of the Marsland Accord and the Earth's transformation as core subjects. Children grow up understanding the importance of environmental stewardship and the interconnectedness of all life forms.

The Green Canopy satellites, once a defensive network, had become the eyes of the galaxy, monitoring the health of planets and providing data crucial for maintaining ecological equilibrium. They were a testament to humanity's ingenuity and a symbol of their commitment to safeguarding the cosmos.

As the New Era unfolded, the UGC celebrated the anniversary of the Marsland Accord with a galaxy-wide festival. It was a time of reflection, gratitude, and renewed commitment to the principles that had brought them all together.

The festival was marked by the planting of the 'Garden of Worlds, a botanical garden on Marsland where flora from every corner of the galaxy was cultivated. It was a living mosaic of the UGC's diversity and a place of peace and contemplation.

The legacy of Marsland and Earth's rebirth continued to inspire countless initiatives. The 'Cosmic Conservatory' was founded, an institution dedicated to the preservation of endangered species and ecosystems across the galaxy.

The New Era was not without its challenges, but the lessons of the past served as a guiding light. The UGC, Earth, and all member worlds stood united, ready to face any obstacle with the wisdom and resolve born from their shared history.

Chapter 13: The Crystal Secrets of Marsland

Marsland's crystal forests were not only a marvel to behold but also a reservoir of cosmic wisdom. The crystalline flora, towering and radiant, had grown from the planet's rich mineral soil, which was imbued with the essence of a comet that had crashed eons ago. These forests were said to hold the secrets of the cosmos, encoded within their multifaceted boughs.

The Comet's Legacy

The comet, known as Kaelum's Tear, was not an ordinary celestial body. It had traversed the universe, absorbing knowledge and energy from the countless worlds it passed. When it collided with Marsland, it didn't bring destruction; instead, it seeded the planet with the potential for life and enlightenment.

The Harmonic Crystals

The crystals of Marsland were unique in their ability to resonate with the natural frequencies of the universe. Scholars from across the galaxies theorized that these vibrations held the patterns of cosmic events—past, present, and future. The UGC established the Marsland Observatory, a research facility dedicated to deciphering these harmonic patterns.

The Guardians of Knowledge

A reclusive order of monks, the Keepers of Kaelum, served as the guardians of the crystal forests. They had developed a symbiotic relationship with the crystals, learning to interpret their resonances and protect their secrets. The Keepers believed that the crystals were sentient, each one a living library of universal lore.

The Synergy of Science and Mysticism

The UGC's scientists, initially skeptical of the Keepers' claims, soon discovered the truth in their words. Advanced instruments detected complex data streams within the crystal frequencies—information aligned with known astrophysical phenomena. This synergy of science and mysticism opened new avenues of research, leading to breakthroughs in interstellar navigation and communication.

The Crystal Conclave

To further explore the potential of the crystal forests, the UGC convened the Crystal Conclave, a gathering of the greatest minds from across the galaxies. The conclave's purpose was to unlock the secrets of the crystals and harness their knowledge for the betterment of all civilizations.

The Revelation

During the conclave, a young Keeper named Lyra unveiled a stunning discovery. By combining the Keepers' ancient techniques with modern technology, she translated a crystal resonance into a visual representation of a distant galaxy. This revelation proved that the crystals were not just passive recorders of information but active observers of the universe.

The Promise of Marsland

The crystal forests of Marsland promised a future where the mysteries of the universe could be unraveled. The UGC once focused solely on governance and conflict resolution and now found itself at the forefront of a cosmic renaissance, with Marsland and its crystal forests at the heart of this new era of discovery.

The Keepers shared their deepest insights into the crystals' nature as the conclave continued. They spoke of the 'Lattice of Light,' an energy network connecting all the crystals, forming a web of consciousness that spanned Marsland. This network was not static; it pulsed with life, responding to the emotions and thoughts of those who walked among the crystal groves.

The UGC's researchers were fascinated by this concept. They began to study the Lattice, finding that it did indeed respond to sentient presence. The crystals glowed brighter in the presence of harmony and dimmed amidst discord, suggesting a level of empathy previously unknown in non-organic entities.

The conclave's work led to the development of the 'Resonance Interface,' a device that allowed direct communication with the crystal network. Through this interface, the Keepers and scientists could ask questions and receive answers in the form of intricate light patterns and vibrations.

The implications were profound. The crystals had witnessed the birth of stars, civilizations' rise and fall, and galaxies' silent dance across the eons. They offered a perspective on the universe that was both ancient and immediate, a view that transcended the limitations of time and space.

As the conclave drew to a close, a ceremony was held within the heart of the crystal forest. The delegates gathered around a particularly large and luminous crystal, which the Keepers called 'The Hearthstone.' Here, they pledged to honor and protect the knowledge of Marsland, to use it wisely, and to share it with all who sought understanding.

The chapter concludes with the Hearthstone emitting a brilliant pulse of light that traveled through the Lattice, reaching every crystal on Marsland. It was a signal of unity and a beacon of shared knowledge, illuminating the path to a future where the secrets of the cosmos would be open to all.

Chapter 14: The Prophecy Unveiled

As the Crystal Conclave delved deeper into the mysteries of Marsland's forests, a profound silence fell upon the assembly. Lyra, the young Keeper, stood before a towering crystal, her hands gently tracing its facets. The air vibrated with anticipation as she initiated the ancient rite of communion, a ritual that allowed a Keeper to attune to the crystal's consciousness.

The crystal pulsed with a soft glow, and a hush descended upon the conclave. Then, with a sudden brilliance, the crystal illuminated the chamber with a vision of Earth's future prophecy that would change the course of history.

The Vision of Tomorrow

The prophecy revealed Earth not as it was but as it could be a world teetering on the brink of two possible futures. In one, Earth was a paradise reborn, its environment thriving and its people living in harmony with nature. On the other, it was a desolate wasteland, a stark warning of what might come to pass if the path of negligence continued.

The Forked Path

The vision depicted a forked path emanating from Earth, each branch representing the choices that lay ahead. One path was bathed in light, lined with verdant trees and clear waters, leading to a future where Earth was a jewel of the galaxy once more. The other was shrouded in darkness, choked with smog and barren landscapes, a testament to the consequences of apathy and greed.

The Guardians' Resolve

The Galactic Guardians, once enforcers, now became protectors of Earth's potential. They pledged to guide humanity along the path of light, offering their strength and wisdom to ensure the brighter future depicted in the prophecy.

Earth's Awakening

The prophecy stirred something deep within the hearts of Earth's inhabitants. It was as if they had been shaken from a long slumber, their eyes now open to the possibilities that lay before them. A global movement, The Pathfinders,' emerged, dedicated to following the prophecy's luminous trail.

The Celestial Alignment

As the prophecy foretold, a celestial event—a rare alignment of planets— would serve as the signpost for Earth's pivotal moment. This alignment would amplify the energies of change, providing a window of opportunity for Earth to set its course firmly on the path of renewal.

The Pledge of the Cosmos

The United Galaxies Council, moved by the prophecy, issued a declaration—the 'Pledge of the Cosmos.' It called upon all civilizations to support Earth in its transformative journey, share knowledge and resources, and stand as witnesses to the dawning of a new era.

Epilogue: The Choice of Ages

The prophecy of the Marsland crystals became a beacon for all of Earth's endeavors. As the celestial alignment approached, the people of Earth united like never before, their actions inspired by the promise of a future filled with hope and beauty.

The choice was theirs to make, and the universe watched with bated breath, ready to welcome Earth as a steward of the galaxy or to mourn its fall into oblivion.

As the conclave absorbed the gravity of the prophecy, discussions erupted on how best to support Earth's journey. The Pathfinders, representing Earth's newfound determination, outlined a series of initiatives designed to align with the prophecy's brighter path. These included global reforestation projects, the phasing out of pollutants, and the adoption of clean energy on a scale never before seen.

In a show of solidarity, the Guardians volunteered to assist in these initiatives, offering their advanced technologies to accelerate Earth's transformation. They also proposed the establishment of the 'Galactic Environmental Corps,' a task force that would respond to ecological crises throughout the galaxy, with Earth as a founding member.

The celestial alignment, drawing nearer with each passing day, became a symbol of hope. Special observatories were constructed to witness the event, and it was declared a galactic holiday. On Earth, people gathered in celebration, their eyes turned skyward, their spirits united by a common dream.

As the planets aligned, a wave of energy washed over Earth, catalyzing the changes that had begun. The atmosphere cleared, the oceans sparkled with renewed life, and the land teemed with diversity. It was as if Earth itself was breathing a sigh of relief, embracing its role as a protector of life.

The chapter concludes with the 'Festival of the Alignment,' a celebration held simultaneously on Earth and Marsland. It was a festival of lights, music, and joy, marking the beginning of a new chapter in the galaxy's history. Earth had made its choice, and the prophecy was fulfilled, not by fate, but by the will of

those who dared to dream of a better
tomorrow.

Chapter 15: The Dawning of the Celestial Event

As the celestial alignment drew near,
Earth's transformation became palpable.
The Pathfinders, a collective of
visionaries and activists, worked
tirelessly to align Earth's actions with
the prophecy. Their efforts were not in
vain, as the once skeptical masses began
to embrace the possibility of a brighter
future.

The Awakening of Terra

The Earth itself seemed to respond to
the impending alignment. Long
dormant natural phenomena awakened
across the planet. Geysers erupted in
joyful plumes, and the auroras danced
with renewed vigor, painting the skies
with hope.

The Harmonic Convergence

The celestial event was more than an astronomical spectacle; it was a harmonic convergence that resonated with the very soul of the universe. As the planets aligned, their energies interwove to create a symphony of cosmic proportions, a melody that sang of new beginnings.

The Crystal Catalyst

Back on Marsland, the crystal forests began to hum with a frequency that permeated space and time. The Keepers of Kaelum, attuned to the crystals' song, declared that the moment of prophecy was at hand. The crystals, they said, were not just revealing Earth's potential future—they were actively participating in its realization.

The Galactic Embrace

The United Galaxies Council, moved by the unfolding events, declared a galaxy-wide day of meditation and reflection. Civilizations across the stars paused in their daily endeavors to focus their collective consciousness on Earth, sending waves of support and encouragement.

The Turning Tide

On Earth, the Pathfinders organized a global event, 'The Day of Alignment,' where billions gathered to witness the celestial spectacle. As the planets reached their perfect configuration, a profound sense of unity swept over the crowds. It was as if the entire planet took a synchronized breath, ready to step into the future.

The Crystal Revelation

At the peak of the alignment, the Marsland crystals shone with ethereal light, casting beams that reached Earth. These beams carried with them the essence of the prophecy, infusing Earth's atmosphere with the potential for change. It was a moment of revelation where every individual felt connected to the greater cosmos.

The Path Forward

With the alignment complete, Earth's leaders and the Pathfinders unveiled 'The Celestial Accord, a new set of guidelines inspired by the prophecy. It outlined a sustainable way of life that balanced technological advancement with environmental stewardship.

Epilogue: The Age of Harmony

The celestial event marked the beginning of the Age of Harmony. Earth, once a cautionary tale, became a testament to the power of unity and the will to change. The prophecy of the Marsland crystals had been fulfilled, not by fate, but by the collective actions of those who dared to dream of a better world.

As the alignment approached, the Pathfinders' message spread like a cosmic wind, reaching every corner of Earth. It whispered of change, of a future where humanity would not only survive but thrive. The message spoke of a time when Earth would not stand alone but would be an integral part of a galactic community, sharing in the wonders and challenges of the cosmos.

The Keepers of Kaelum, in their crystal sanctuaries, prepared for the alignment with rituals that dated back millennia. They chanted in ancient tongues, their voices harmonizing with the crystals, amplifying the energy that flowed through Marsland's veins.

Many civilizations reflected on their journeys, triumphs, and failures during the Galactic Embrace and considered how they could contribute to the tapestry of galactic life. Many sent emissaries to Earth, offering gifts of knowledge and pledges of friendship.

The Turning Tide was not just a momentary event but the start of a wave that would carry Earth forward for generations. The Day of Alignment saw humanity's collective spirit soar. People from all walks of life, from the highest leaders to the humblest citizens, stood side by side, gazing skyward as the planets traced their celestial dance.

The Crystal Revelation was not confined to the visual spectacle. It was a more profound awakening, a realization that every person had a role to play in the unfolding story of Earth. The beams from Marsland's crystals touched more than the atmosphere; they touched the hearts and minds of all who witnessed them.

The Path Forward was laid out in 'The Celestial Accord,' a document that became Earth's new constitution for living. It was a promise to future generations that the beauty and diversity of the Earth would be preserved and that the mistakes of the past would not be repeated.

The Age of Harmony was heralded by celebrations that spanned the globe. Monuments were erected to commemorate the alignment, each symbolizing Earth's commitment to the path set forth by the prophecy.

The chapter concludes with a scene of Earth, a blue and green gem hanging in the vastness of space, its surface dotted with lights that signified the unity of its people. The celestial alignment had passed, but its influence would be felt forever. Earth had stepped into the Age of Harmony, ready to embrace its destiny among the stars.

Chapter 16: The Legacy of the Alignment

The celestial alignment had passed, but its legacy was beginning to unfold. Earth had entered a new epoch where the harmony between technology and nature was not just an ideal but a reality. The Age of Harmony, as it came to be known, was marked by a series of groundbreaking developments that would define Earth's future and its place in the cosmos.

The Green Revolution

The first sign of the new age was the Green Revolution. Innovations in clean energy and sustainable living spread like wildfire across the planet. Cities transformed into living ecosystems, with vertical gardens scaling skyscrapers and transportation systems powered by renewable sources.

The Crystal Technology Exchange

In a historic decision, the Keepers of Kaelum agreed to share the secrets of the Marsland crystals with Earth's scientists. This exchange led to the development of crystal-based technologies that revolutionized communication, energy storage, and even medical treatments.

The Intergalactic Alliance

The United Galaxies Council, inspired by Earth's transformation, formed the Intergalactic Alliance, a coalition dedicated to the preservation and advancement of all life forms. Earth was invited as a founding member, a testament to its newfound commitment to interstellar stewardship.

The Guardians' New Mission

The Galactic Guardians, once feared enforcers, were reformed into the Guardians of Harmony. Their new mission was to safeguard the peace and ecological balance of the galaxy, intervening only to aid planets in nurturing their environments.

The Cultural Renaissance

A renaissance of arts and culture blossomed on Earth, fueled by the newfound connection with the cosmos. Music, literature, and visual arts drew inspiration from the stars, celebrating the unity of galactic civilizations and the beauty of the universe.

The Cosmic Voyage

Humanity's age-old dream of exploring the stars became a reality. The first interstellar voyage, the 'Harmony Expedition, set out to explore and learn from distant worlds. The expedition symbolized Earth's role as an explorer and learner rather than a conqueror.

The Prophecy's Continuation

The Marsland crystals, now in a symbiotic relationship with Earth, continued to reveal insights into the fabric of the cosmos. A new prophecy emerged one that spoke of an era of enlightenment spreading across the galaxies, with Earth as its beacon.

The Harmonic Epoch

As centuries turned to millennia, the Age of Harmony grew into the Harmonic Epoch. Earth's journey from the brink of destruction to a leader in cosmic unity was remembered as a pivotal chapter in the galaxy's annals. The legacy of the celestial alignment lived on, a reminder that even the smallest of changes can echo throughout the universe.

The Age of Harmony also saw the rise of the 'Eco-Architects,' visionaries who reshaped urban landscapes. They designed self-sustaining buildings and public spaces that not only met human needs but also contributed to the health of the planet. These structures were equipped with solar skins, wind turbines, and rainwater harvesting systems, making each building a standalone ecosystem.

The Crystal Technology Exchange flourished as the Marsland crystals became a cornerstone of Earth's technological renaissance. These crystals, once enigmatic and untapped, were now part of everyday life, powering devices and machinery with an efficiency that surpassed all conventional means.

The Intergalactic Alliance grew in strength and number, with Earth playing a crucial role in its expansion. The Alliance's charter was not limited to environmental issues; it also addressed social and economic disparities, aiming to create a galaxy where every being had the opportunity to thrive.

The Guardians of Harmony embarked on missions that were once unimaginable. They restored ravaged worlds, reversed ecological disasters, and even prevented conflicts that threatened planetary ecosystems. Their presence became a symbol of hope and a promise of assistance to all who needed it.

The Cultural Renaissance on Earth had a profound effect on the galaxy at large. Earth's art and music transcended cultural and linguistic barriers, becoming beloved throughout the United Galaxies. The 'Interstellar Art Festival, hosted on Earth, became a celebrated event, drawing participants from every corner of the cosmos.

The Harmony Expedition was the first of many. It paved the way for a new age of exploration, where the focus was on understanding and learning from the vastness of space. The expeditions were not conquests but journeys of discovery, with each returning ship bringing back knowledge that benefited all.

The new prophecy revealed by the Marsland crystals spoke of a time when the barriers between worlds would dissolve, not just physically but spiritually. It foretold an era where the consciousness of the galaxy would rise to a new level of understanding and empathy.

The Harmonic Epoch was not just a period of peace; it was an era of growth and enlightenment. The lessons learned from Earth's past mistakes and the prophecy's guidance shaped a more connected and conscious galaxy than ever before.

The chapter concludes with a panoramic view of Earth, a vibrant oasis in the void of space, its blue oceans, and green lands, a testament to the enduring spirit of its inhabitants. The celestial alignment was a distant memory, but its influence continued to guide the destiny of Earth and its people, a beacon of harmony in the cosmic sea.

Chapter 17: The Galactic Response to Earth's Metamorphosis

Earth's transformation into a beacon of sustainability and harmony sent ripples throughout the cosmos. Civilizations across the galaxies are observed with a mix of astonishment, admiration, and inspiration. The Age of Harmony was not just an Earthly phenomenon; it became a galactic milestone.

The Zephyrians' Enlightenment

The Zephyrians, once skeptics of Earth's potential, found themselves humbled by the planet's resurgence. Their gaseous forms, which had undulated with doubt, now shimmered with the colors of respect. They sent emissaries to Earth, seeking to learn the art of ecological balance and to share their own knowledge of atmospheric regeneration.

The Andromedans' Alliance

The Andromedans, led by President Xylo-Thorax, extended their hand in partnership. They offered Earth a place in the Andromedan Consortium, a collective dedicated to technological and cultural exchange. Earth's art, music, and literature found new audiences among the stars, while Andromedan technology helped Earthlings explore the far reaches of space.

The Sirians' Sympathy

The Sirians, water beings from the Sirius system, were deeply moved by Earth's commitment to reviving its oceans. They initiated the 'Blue Bonds' project, a joint venture to protect aquatic ecosystems galaxy-wide. Earth's efforts sparked a conservation movement that transcended planetary boundaries.

The Centaurians' Collaboration

The Centaurians, known for their advanced agricultural systems, reached out to share their techniques for sustainable farming. Together with Earth's agronomists, they developed hybrid methods that increased food production while preserving natural resources, ensuring food security for Earth and beyond.

The Orion's Overture

The Orions, master builders of the galaxy, marveled at Earth's architectural revolution. They invited Earth's architects and engineers to the Orion Belt to collaborate on constructing eco-cities that could house billions without harming the environment.

The Pleiadians' Peace

The Pleiadians, spiritual guides of the Pleiades cluster, embraced Earth's cultural renaissance. They saw Earth's journey as a testament to the power of peace and proposed the 'Harmonic Convergence Festivals,' celebrated galaxy-wide to honor unity and diversity.

The Vega's Vision

The Vegans, visionaries from the Vega star, were inspired by Earth's Green Canopy satellites. They proposed the 'Stellar Network,' a system of satellites designed to monitor and maintain the health of planets across the Milky Way.

Epilogue: The Cosmic Congregation

The transformation of Earth had become a catalyst for a new era of interstellar cooperation. The United Galaxies Council, once a forum for debate and decision-making, evolved into a congregation of cultures, species, and worlds, all united by a common vision of a harmonious and sustainable universe.

The galactic response was a symphony of initiatives and collaborations. The Zephyrians, with their newfound respect for Earth, established the 'Zephyr Exchange Program, allowing Earth's environmentalists to study their advanced atmospheric technologies. In return, Earth shared its breakthroughs in renewable energy, which were particularly well-suited to the Zephyrians' floating cities.

The Andromedan Consortium became a melting pot of ideas and creativity. Earth's membership brought a fresh perspective to the group, sparking a cultural renaissance that rippled through Andromeda's many systems. The exchange of art and science fostered a deeper understanding between the two civilizations, bridging gaps that had once seemed insurmountable.

The 'Blue Bonds' project became a model for interstellar environmentalism. The Sirians, with their innate connection to water, found kinship with Earth's oceanographers and marine biologists. Together, they charted new courses for conservation, ensuring the vitality of aquatic life on both Earth and Sirius.

The Centaurians' collaboration with Earth's farmers led to the 'Green Harvest Initiative,' a program that revolutionized agriculture across the galaxy. The initiative combined Centaurian techniques with Earth's permaculture practices, creating sustainable food systems that could feed billions without depleting planetary resources.

The Orion Belt witnessed the rise of new cities, designed and built with

Earth's help. These cities were marvels of sustainability, blending Orion engineering with Earth's ecological principles. The collaboration was a testament to what could be achieved when two civilizations shared a common goal of harmony with nature.

The Pleiadians' Harmonic Convergence Festivals' became a staple of galactic culture. These festivals were not just celebrations but also forums for peace talks and diplomatic relations. Earth's journey from discord to harmony inspired many worlds to seek peaceful resolutions to their conflicts.

The 'Stellar Network' proposed by the Vegans was a visionary project that expanded on the concept of Earth's Green Canopy. It became a galaxy-spanning web of satellites that monitored the health of planets, providing early warnings for ecological imbalances and facilitating swift responses to environmental threats.

The Cosmic Congregation marked a new chapter in the annals of the galaxy. The United Galaxies Council, with Earth as a prominent member, became a beacon of unity. It was a place where voices from across the stars came together to share wisdom, forge alliances, and ensure the prosperity of all life forms.

The chapter concludes with a panoramic view of the Milky Way, a tapestry of worlds and civilizations, each shining with its own light yet connected by the shared vision of a sustainable future. Earth, once a silent observer, was now a vibrant participant in the cosmic dance, its metamorphosis a testament to the power of change and the strength of unity.

Chapter 18: The Shadow Stirring

In the far reaches of the Andromeda Galaxy, a rogue faction known as the 'Eclipse Syndicate' emerged from the shadows. Discontent with the new era of peace and cooperation, they yearned for the old days of chaos and power struggles. The Syndicate believed that conflict was the true catalyst for evolution and innovation.

The Syndicate's Creed

The Eclipse Syndicate was a coalition of dissidents, outcasts, and radicals who shared a common ideology—that strength was forged in the fires of adversity. They saw the galactic harmony as a stagnation, a lull that dulled the survival instincts of civilizations.

The Disruption Begins

The Syndicate launched a series of covert operations, aiming to destabilize the pillars of peace. They spread propaganda, incited unrest, and sabotaged key infrastructures. Their actions were subtle, designed to sow seeds of doubt and fear without revealing their presence.

The Galactic Guardians' Dilemma

The Guardians of Harmony faced a new challenge. Their mission had always been to protect and aid, but now they were up against an invisible enemy. They had to adapt to become defenders against the darkness that sought to engulf the light of harmony.

The Council's Response

The United Galaxies Council convened an emergency session to address the rising threat. They knew that a direct confrontation might play into the

Syndicate's hands, sparking the very conflict they sought to avoid. A different approach was needed—one that preserved the unity of the galaxies while rooting out the malevolent force.

The Silent War

A silent war waged in the shadows of the cosmos. The Syndicate's moves were met with countermeasures by the Council's elite operatives, known as the 'Star Sentinels.' These Sentinels worked tirelessly to dismantle the Syndicate's schemes while maintaining the facade of peace.

The Turning Point

The Syndicate's overreach came when they attempted to corrupt the Marsland crystals. The Keepers of Kaelum, sensing the disturbance, alerted the Council. The Sentinels, alongside the Keepers, launched a daring mission to protect the crystals and expose the Syndicate's machinations.

The Eclipse's End

The mission was a success. The Syndicate's leaders were captured, and their plots were laid bare before the galaxies. The Council offered the Syndicate a choice—join the harmonious society they had sought to destroy or be exiled to the fringes of space.

Epilogue: The Harmony Preserved

The Eclipse Syndicate's fall served as a stark reminder that peace must be actively maintained. The galaxies learned that harmony was not a static state but a dynamic balance that required vigilance and resolve. The Age of Harmony continued, stronger and more united than ever, with the shadow of the Syndicate serving as a cautionary tale for the future.

The Syndicate's creed, once a rallying cry for the disenchanted, became a symbol of misguided ambition. Their belief in adversity as a crucible for strength was not entirely without merit, but their methods were flawed, rooted in a past that the galaxy had outgrown.

The disruptions caused by the Syndicate were not merely physical; they were ideological. Their propaganda tapped into deep-seated fears and insecurities, challenging the convictions of many who had embraced the Age of Harmony. Yet, in the face of this ideological assault, the galactic community stood firm, their resolve unshaken.

The Guardians of Harmony, in their new role, became beacons of hope. They demonstrated that strength did not come from conflict but from the courage to protect and preserve. Their adaptation to the Syndicate's shadowy tactics was a testament to their unwavering commitment to peace.

The Council's response to the Syndicate's threat was measured and strategic. They understood that the true battle was not against a visible enemy but against the seeds of discord that the Syndicate had sown. Their approach was one of healing and reconciliation, not retribution.

The silent war, though unseen by most, was felt throughout the cosmos. The Star Sentinels, in their clandestine operations, ensured that the Syndicate's attempts to undermine the peace were thwarted at every turn. Their actions, though covert, were crucial in preserving the fabric of galactic society.

The turning point in the conflict came with the Syndicate's attempt to manipulate the Marsland crystals. This act of desecration united the galaxies against them, turning any who might have sympathized with their cause away from their darkness.

The Eclipse's end marked a new beginning for the galaxy. The Syndicate's leaders, once defiant, were now faced with the consequences of their actions. The choice given to them by the Council was a reflection of the Age of Harmony's principles—offering a path to redemption rather than exile and isolation.

The epilogue of the Syndicate's tale was a lesson in vigilance. The galaxies recognized that the price of peace was eternal mindfulness and that the shadow of conflict would always lurk at the edges of the light. Yet, they moved forward, undeterred, their spirits bolstered by the knowledge that together, they could overcome any challenge.

The chapter concludes with a renewed sense of purpose among the stars. The Age of Harmony, strengthened by the trials it had faced, shone brighter than ever. The legacy of the celestial alignment, and the shadow it had cast, would forever remind the galaxies that harmony was a treasure to be cherished and protected.

Chapter 19: The Unseen Wisdom

The fall of the Eclipse Syndicate brought a period of introspection across the galaxies. The Council, in their victory, pondered the ideology that had driven the Syndicate to such lengths. What if, within the darkness of their actions, there lay a kernel of truth?

The Ideology Reexamined

The Syndicate's belief in conflict as a catalyst for evolution resonated with some. It raised questions about the nature of progress and the role of adversity in fostering strength and innovation. The Council formed a committee to delve into these ideas, seeking to understand rather than condemn.

The Doctrine of Dualities

The committee's research led to the Doctrine of Dualities, a philosophy that recognized the interplay between harmony and discord. It posited that true progress required a balance—too much harmony could lead to complacency, while too much conflict could lead to destruction.

The Syndicate's Legacy

The Syndicate, though misguided in their methods, had inadvertently highlighted the need for challenge and growth. The Council decided to honor this unintended legacy by establishing the 'Galactic Challenges, a series of peaceful competitions and simulations designed to stimulate innovation and resilience without resorting to conflict.

The Guardians' New Quest

The Guardians of Harmony embraced their new role in overseeing the Galactic

Challenges. They ensured that these events were conducted with integrity and that the spirit of competition served to unite rather than divide.

The Rebirth of the Syndicate

The remnants of the Syndicate were given a choice: join the new initiative and channel their beliefs into constructive challenges or remain in exile. Many chose redemption, bringing their fierce drive and sharp intellects to the Galactic Challenges, where they became champions of progress.

The Harmonic Balance

The galaxies began to thrive under the Doctrine of Dualities. Civilizations engaged in galactic challenges, pushing the boundaries of science, art, and philosophy. The balance between harmony and adversity fostered a dynamic society that was ever-evolving yet stable.

The Crystal Confluence

The Marsland crystals, sensitive to the shifts in the cosmos, began to resonate with a new frequency. This frequency was neither the calm hum of harmony nor the discordant pulse of conflict but a complex melody that spoke of balance and growth.

Epilogue: The Symphony of the Stars

The hidden truth within the Syndicate's ideology had been revealed and transformed. The galaxies now danced to the Symphony of the Stars, a cosmic composition that celebrated the duality of existence. The Age of Harmony had matured into the Era of Dynamic Equilibrium, where every being played a part in the grand chorus of the universe.

The Doctrine of Dualities became a cornerstone of galactic philosophy. It was taught in schools, debated by philosophers, and even influenced policy-making. The doctrine suggested that adversity in controlled measures could be a powerful ally in the quest for advancement.

The Galactic Challenges became a celebrated tradition, with events ranging from intellectual debates to technological exhibitions. These challenges were broadcast throughout the galaxies, inspiring innovation and fostering a sense of camaraderie among diverse civilizations.

The Guardians of Harmony found a new purpose in their quest. They became mentors and facilitators, guiding participants through the challenges and ensuring that the spirit of competition remained healthy and constructive.

The Syndicate's rebirth was a tale of redemption. Those who had once sought to undermine the peace now stood as its staunchest advocates. Their transformation was a testament to the

Council's wisdom in choosing to rehabilitate rather than punishment.

The Harmonic Balance ushered in an era of unprecedented prosperity. Civilizations flourished, and the exchange of ideas and resources became the norm. The balance acted as a catalyst, driving societies to reach new heights while maintaining the integrity of their cultures and ecosystems.

The Crystal Confluence revealed new layers of cosmic knowledge. The Keepers of Kaelum, working with scientists, unraveled complex cosmic patterns that had implications for understanding the nature of the universe and the forces that governed it.

The Symphony of the Stars became the anthem of an enlightened age. It was a symphony composed of every action, thought, and emotional melody woven into the fabric of reality, harmonizing the planets' dance and stars' pulse.

The Era of Dynamic Equilibrium was marked by a profound understanding that growth and stability were not mutually exclusive. The galaxies embraced the ebb and flow of change, secure in the knowledge that the harmony they cherished would guide them through the ages.

The chapter concludes with a vision of the future, where the Symphony of the Stars resonates in the heart of every being. The galaxies, once disparate and isolated, now move together in a grand cosmic ballet, each step reflecting the wisdom gleaned from the shadows and the light.

Chapter 20: The Redemption Quest

The leader of the Eclipse Syndicate, known only as Cipher, emerged from the shadows of defeat with a singular purpose: redemption. Cipher, once the architect of chaos, now sought to mend the rifts his actions had caused. He proposed an impossible challenge that would test the limits of his intellect and the depth of his resolve.

Cipher's Pledge

Cipher approached the United Galaxies Council with a pledge to undertake a quest that many deemed unattainable—to traverse the 'Labyrinth of Infinity,' a cosmic maze that twisted through dimensions and time. It was said that at the heart of the labyrinth lay the 'Orb of Unity,' an artifact of immense power that could bind or unravel the fabric of the cosmos.

The Council's Deliberation

The Council, intrigued by Cipher's proposal, agreed to his quest under one condition: he would be accompanied by a team of representatives from various civilizations, ensuring that his journey was for the greater good. The team, known as the 'Harmony Brigade, would assist Cipher and safeguard the Orb of Unity.

The Labyrinth's Legacy

The Labyrinth of Infinity was an enigma believed to be the creation of an ancient, advanced civilization. Its purpose was unclear, but legends spoke of it as a trial, a test of worthiness for those who dared to seek its heart.

The Journey Commences

Cipher and the Harmony Brigade embarked on their journey, equipped with the knowledge and technology of a thousand worlds. The labyrinth challenged them with puzzles that spanned quantum mechanics, astrophysics, and the very essence of life. Each trial was a reflection of the Syndicate's ideology, forcing Cipher to confront the consequences of his past actions.

The Trials of Redemption

As they delved deeper into the labyrinth, the trials grew more complex and perilous. The Brigade faced illusions that tested their perceptions, paradoxes that defied logic, and echoes of time that threatened to trap them in eternal loops.

The Heart of the Maze

After what seemed like an eternity, Cipher and the Brigade reached the heart of the labyrinth. The Orb of Unity hovered before them, pulsating with a light that seemed to contain the universe itself. Cipher, standing before the Orb, realized that the true challenge was not reaching it, but understanding its purpose.

The Orb's Revelation

Cipher reached out to the Orb, and in a moment of clarity, he understood. The labyrinth was not a test of intellect or strength but of harmony. The Orb of

Unity did not hold power over the cosmos—it was a mirror, reflecting the unity of those who sought it.

The Return

With the Orb's wisdom, Cipher and the Brigade emerged from the labyrinth transformed. They returned to the Council with a message: the greatest challenges cannot be conquered alone but with the combined strength and wisdom of many.

Epilogue: The Symphony Resonates

Cipher's quest for redemption became a legend, a story told across the galaxies. It served as a reminder that even those who wander in darkness can find their way back to the light through unity and cooperation.

The Redemption Quest was more than a journey through space; it was a voyage through the soul. Cipher, once a harbinger of discord, now sought to weave a tapestry of concord. His transformation was a testament to the belief that anyone could change, no matter what their past.

Cipher's Transformation

Throughout the quest, Cipher's transformation became evident to all. His once cold and calculating demeanor gave way to empathy and understanding. The Harmony Brigade, initially wary of their former adversary, grew to respect the man who had once been their nemesis.

The Labyrinth's Lessons

The Labyrinth of Infinity taught them all invaluable lessons. It was a crucible that forged their spirits in the fires of trials. Each puzzle solved and each paradox untangled brought them closer, not just to the Orb, but to each other.

The Echoes of Time

The echoes of time they encountered were not mere obstacles; they were reflections of potential futures, each shaped by the actions of the Brigade. These temporal mirages underscored the importance of the choices they made, not just for themselves, but for the continuum of history.

The Orb's Custodians

Upon their return, the Harmony Brigade became the Orb's custodians, its guardians. They understood that the Orb's power was not to be wielded but to be shared—a symbol of the collective wisdom of the galaxies.

The Council's Evolution

The United Galaxies Council, inspired by Cipher's journey, evolved. They became not just a governing body, but a beacon of enlightenment, guiding other civilizations through their own dark times.

The Symphony of Redemption

The Symphony of Redemption, as Cipher's quest came to be known, was a melody composed of courage, change, and the indomitable will to do better. It played across the stars, a harmonious tune that reminded all of the power of redemption.

The Dawn of Understanding

The galaxies stood at the dawn of understanding, looking towards a future where the shadows of the past were lessons for a brighter tomorrow. The Redemption Quest was a catalyst for this new era, an era where wisdom was the greatest currency and unity the strongest force.

The chapter concludes with Cipher, once a shadow, now a beacon of light, standing before the Council. His eyes, once filled with the fire of conquest, now glowed with the warmth of fellowship.

His quest had changed him, the galaxies, and the course of history forever.

Chapter 21: The Echoes of the Labyrinth

As Cipher and the Harmony Brigade navigated the Labyrinth of Infinity, Earth's ecosystems began to resonate with the trials faced within. It was as if the labyrinth extended its reach beyond space's confines, touching the essence of Earth's life force.

The Whispering Forests

The ancient forests of Earth whispered among themselves, their leaves rustling with the echoes of the labyrinth's puzzles. Each challenge overcome by the Brigade was mirrored by a burst of growth and vitality within the woods. Trees grew stronger, their roots delving deeper into the soil, intertwining in a complex network that mirrored the intricate pathways of the labyrinth.

The Singing Oceans

The oceans sang with the harmonies of the labyrinth's trials. As the Brigade solved riddles of fluid dynamics and navigated temporal streams, the tides on Earth responded. New currents formed, cleansing the waters and bringing life to once-barren depths. Marine creatures thrived; their movements synchronized with the ebb and flow of the labyrinth's energy.

The Dancing Deserts

The deserts of Earth, often seen as places of desolation, began to dance with life. The sands shifted, revealing hidden oases as Cipher and the Brigade unlocked secrets of survival and adaptation. Cacti bloomed with unprecedented colors, and creatures of the arid lands reveled in the newfound abundance.

The Soaring Skies

The skies above Earth soared with the Brigade's progress through the labyrinth. Birds took flight in patterns that traced the celestial paths deciphered by the team. The atmosphere itself seemed to clear, the air fresh with the promise of new beginnings, reflecting the clarity of thought achieved within the labyrinth's walls.

The Vigilant Mountains

The mountains stood vigilant, their peaks reaching towards the stars. As the Brigade faced challenges of strength and endurance, the mountains echoed their resolve. Rock formations shifted, creating natural sculptures that stood as monuments to the trials within the labyrinth.

The Resonant Ice

The polar ice caps, sensitive to the slightest change, resonated with the labyrinth's essence. Glaciers, which had been retreating, began to stabilize, their meltwater feeding rivers and lakes. The ice whispered of the delicate balance between permanence and change, a lesson learned by Cipher in the heart of the maze.

The Orb's Influence

Once secured by the Brigade, the Orb of Unity amplified Earth's response to the labyrinth. Its energy pulsed through the planet, enhancing the symbiotic relationships between species and their environments. Earth's ecosystems were not just reacting but evolving, becoming more resilient and interconnected.

Epilogue: The Living Labyrinth

The labyrinth's challenges had become a catalyst for Earth's ecological renaissance. The planet itself had become a living labyrinth, a testament to the power of unity and the strength found in diversity. Earth's once-threatened ecosystems now flourished, a mirror to the harmony achieved by Cipher and the Harmony Brigade in their quest for redemption.

The Echoes of the Labyrinth resonated beyond the physical realm, touching the consciousness of Earth's inhabitants. People reported dreams filled with intricate patterns and puzzles, inspiring them to create, innovate, and solve problems in their waking lives.

The Dreaming Jungles

In the tropics, the jungles dreamt along with the people. Vines and lianas wove themselves into natural labyrinths, while flowers bloomed in patterns that reflected the cosmic geometry of the labyrinth. Wildlife, too, has adapted, developing new ways to navigate and thrive in the ever-changing environment.

The Murmuring Plains

The vast plains murmured tales of the labyrinth's influence. Grasses swayed in rhythmic patterns, and herd migrations traced paths that mimicked the maze's winding routes. The plains became a canvas painted with the story of the labyrinth's reach.

The Orb's Echo

The Orb of Unity, now in harmony with Earth, sent echoes of its presence across the planet. These echoes were not sounds but energy waves that inspired unity and collaboration among Earth's diverse cultures and nations.

The Harmony Brigade's Legacy

Upon their return, the Harmony Brigade was hailed as heroes. They shared their experiences, teaching the lessons of the labyrinth to all who would listen. Their journey became a symbol of Earth's potential, a narrative of overcoming adversity through unity and collective wisdom.

The Labyrinth's Continuum

Though left behind in the depths of space, the Labyrinth of Infinity continued to influence Earth. It had become a part of the planet's mythology, a story to challenge and inspire future generations.

The Living Labyrinth's Growth

Earth, the Living Labyrinth, grew in complexity and beauty. Its ecosystems, now interwoven with the energy of the Orb, reached a new equilibrium. This equilibrium was dynamic, ever-shifting, and adapting, much like the labyrinth that had inspired it.

The chapter concludes with Earth standing as a testament to the transformative power of unity. The Echoes of the Labyrinth had become a symphony of life, a melody that played across the verdant fields, beneath the rolling waves, and within the hearts of all who called Earth home.

Chapter 22: The Fork in the Cosmic Road

The labyrinth's trials revealed a profound truth: every choice made by an individual, a civilization, or a galaxy has cosmic consequences. The paths taken and those forsaken resonate through the fabric of the universe, shaping realities and destinies.

The Path of Light

Choosing the path of light, as Earth did, led to an era of unprecedented growth and harmony. This choice reverberated across the cosmos, inspiring other civilizations to follow suit. The Galactic Challenges became a celebration of this choice, fostering innovation and unity without conflict.

The Path of Shadows

Conversely, had Earth chosen the path of shadows, embracing the Syndicate's ideology of chaos and power, the consequences would have been dire. The delicate balance of the cosmos might have tilted towards discord, with civilizations turning inward, driven by fear and a desire for self-preservation.

The Ripple Effect

Each path chosen created ripples that affected not just the immediate environment but also distant worlds and future generations. The path of light strengthened the bonds between galaxies, leading to a golden age of cooperation. The path of shadows could have unraveled these bonds, leading to isolation and stagnation.

The Universal Tapestry

The cosmos is a tapestry woven from the threads of countless decisions. The labyrinth served as a loom, with Cipher and the Harmony Brigade's choices weaving patterns of light and dark. Their journey through the maze was a microcosm of the larger cosmic dance of choices and consequences.

The Balance of Choices

The Doctrine of Dualities acknowledged that both paths held value. The path of light was necessary for peace and growth, while the path of shadows, when not taken to extremes, could serve as a reminder of the importance of resilience and vigilance.

The Echoes of Marsland

The Marsland crystals, ever attuned to the universe's frequencies, captured the echoes of these paths. They sang of the beauty of the path of light and whispered cautionary tales of the path of shadows, ensuring that the wisdom of both was preserved.

The Guardians' Vigil

The Guardians of Harmony, now aware of the weight of their choices, stood vigilant. They became the keepers of the path, guiding those who strayed toward the light and offering counsel to those tempted by the shadows.

Epilogue: The Cosmic Crossroads

The labyrinth's legacy was a universe at a crossroads, with each civilization holding the power to choose its path. The cosmic consequences of these choices would continue to shape the fabric of reality in a never-ending journey through the stars.

The Path of Light shone as a beacon, guiding civilizations toward a future where collaboration and understanding were the cornerstones of society. The Galactic Challenges, once a platform for competition, transformed into a stage for shared triumphs and collective advancements.

The Shadow's Lesson

Though not chosen, the Path of Shadows remained a stark reminder of the potential for downfall. It served as a lesson that peace and harmony were treasures to be actively maintained, not passive states to be taken for granted.

The Cosmic Echo

The Ripple Effect of Earth's choice became known as the Cosmic Echo, a phenomenon that touched the lives of beings in far-off galaxies. It inspired movements similar to Earth's Green Revolution, leading to a wave of ecological and social reforms across the stars.

The Woven Destiny

The Universal Tapestry continued to expand, with new threads added by the choices of countless beings. The labyrinth's influence was evident in the intricate patterns that emerged, a complex yet harmonious blend of light and dark.

The Duality Embraced

The Balance of Choices became a guiding principle for many. Civilizations recognized that challenges and adversities were opportunities for growth, and they sought to face them with the same courage and unity that Cipher and the Harmony Brigade had shown.

The Crystal's Song

The Echoes of Marsland resonated with the stories of those who walked the path of light and those who learned from the shadows. The crystals' song became a symphony of experiences, a collective memory of the universe's journey.

The Vigilant Watch

The Guardians' Vigil evolved into a proactive pursuit of potential threats and a nurturing hand for emerging civilizations. They became ambassadors of the Doctrine of Dualities, teaching the importance of balance and the strength found in diversity.

The Crossroads Embraced

The Epilogue: The Cosmic Crossroads saw the universe embracing its multitude of choices. Civilizations came together at the crossroads, sharing their experiences and learning from one another. The labyrinth's legacy had become a shared heritage, a common history that united the stars.

The chapter concludes with a vision of the cosmos as a living entity, pulsating with the choices of its inhabitants. The paths of light and shadows intertwined, creating a road that was ever-changing, ever-growing a cosmic road that led to infinite possibilities.

Chapter 23: The Shadow Council's Gambit

In the underbelly of Earth's rejuvenated cities, a clandestine assembly of industrial magnates—the Shadow Council—convened. Discontent with the new world order under the UGC Accord, they plotted to reclaim the power and influence they had lost in the Age of Harmony.

The Council's Conspiracy

The Shadow Council was a mosaic of Earth's most powerful industrialists, who had thrived in the era of unchecked capitalism. They saw the UGC's environmental and social reforms as shackles on their ambitions. In secret, they forged alliances with radical groups across the political spectrum, offering financial support to sow discord and incite revolution.

The Seeds of Sedition

Fueled by the Shadow Council's resources, the radicals launched a series of uprisings. Protests erupted in city squares, and digital campaigns flooded the infosphere. The industrialists' goal was to destabilize the governments that had embraced the UGC's vision, hoping to install puppet regimes that would serve their interests.

The Guardians' Dilemma

The Guardians of Harmony, once protectors of ecological balance, now faced a threat from within. They were torn between intervening in Earth's internal affairs and respecting the sovereignty that had been the cornerstone of the UGC Accord.

The Council's Response

The United Galaxies Council, upon learning of the Shadow Council's machinations, was forced to reevaluate its stance. They could not allow the seeds of chaos to take root on Earth again, but direct intervention risked validating the industrialists' claims of UGC overreach.

The Silent Sentinels

The Star Sentinels, the Council's covert operatives, were dispatched to Earth. Their mission is to infiltrate the Shadow Council and dismantle their network from within. They worked alongside Earth's intelligence agencies, unraveling the web of corruption and deceit.

The Turning Tide

As the truth of the Shadow Council's conspiracy came to light, public opinion turned against them. The radicals, realizing they had been pawns in a larger game, withdrew their support. The industrialists found themselves isolated, their influence waning.

The New Dawn

The failed coup became a catalyst for further reforms on Earth. The governments, bolstered by the people's mandate, enacted new laws to prevent the concentration of power and ensure that the few would not dictate the planet's future.

Epilogue: The Triumph of Unity

The Shadow Council's gambit had backfired, serving only to strengthen the resolve of Earth's citizens. The Age of Harmony was reaffirmed, not through suppression, but through the collective will of a society that had chosen a path of light over the shadows of the past.

The Shadow Council's gambit, a dark echo of the past, became a lesson for the future. Their conspiracy, though dangerous, reminded the citizens of Earth of the vigilance required to maintain their hard-won peace.

The Undercurrents of Dissent

The undercurrents of dissent that the Shadow Council had hoped to exploit instead became channels for dialogue and reform. The uprisings they incited led to open forums where citizens and governments came together to address grievances and build a more inclusive society.

The Guardians' Resolve

In their new dilemma, the Guardians of Harmony found strength in restraint. They chose to support Earth's own institutions, providing guidance and intelligence rather than direct intervention, a decision that reinforced Earth's sovereignty and self-determination.

The Council's Wisdom

The United Galaxies Council's response to the Shadow Council's threat was a testament to their wisdom. They understood that the true strength of the UGC Accord lay in its ability to inspire and empower, not to dominate and control.

The Sentinels' Shadow Dance

The Silent Sentinels, the unsung heroes of this tale, danced a shadowy ballet with the agents of the Shadow Council. Their silent war was one of wits and cunning, fought in the hidden corners of cyberspace and the back alleys of power.

The Dawn of Transparency

The New Dawn brought with it a wave of transparency and accountability. Governments, once distant and opaque, opened their doors to the people, inviting them to participate in the process of governance and policy-making.

The Unity's Triumph

The Epilogue: The Triumph of Unity celebrated the collective spirit and reaffirmed that the Age of Harmony was not a static achievement but a living, breathing ideal that required constant nurturing and defense.

The chapter concludes with Earth standing resilient, a world united not just by laws and treaties but by the shared conviction of its people. The Shadow Council's gambit, a specter of the old ways, had dissolved into the light of a new day, where unity and cooperation were the cornerstones of a thriving planet.

Chapter 24: The Shadow Council's Gambit – Continued

Fueled by the Shadow Council's machinations, the revolution plunged Earth into turmoil. The once-thriving ecosystems began to wither as the pillars of society crumbled. Hunger and scarcity ravaged the lands, and the specter of desolation loomed over humanity.

The Descent into Chaos

As the Shadow Council's influence grew, its tactics became more ruthless. It exploited the chaos, manipulating the media and resources to turn the people against each other and their governments. The streets, once filled with harmonious melodies of unity, now echoed with the cries of strife and despair.

The Ravaged Earth

The industrialists' relentless pursuit of power led to the exploitation of Earth's natural resources, pushing the planet to the brink. The delicate balance that had been restored was now under threat as the Shadow Council sought to undo the progress of the Age of Harmony.

The Spread of Hunger

The disruption of supply chains and the destruction of arable land led to widespread hunger. The Shadow Council hoarded food and water, using them as leverage to bend the desperate populace to their will.

The Guardians' Struggle

The Guardians of Harmony, once symbols of peace, now faced their greatest challenge. They had to navigate the fine line between intervention and respect for Earth's autonomy, all while combating the Shadow Council's subterfuge.

The Council's Countermeasure

The United Galaxies Council, recognizing the gravity of the situation, launched a covert operation to support Earth's resistance. The Star Sentinels worked alongside Earth's remaining loyal forces to undermine the Shadow Council's operations.

The Turning of the Tide

The tide began to turn when the people of Earth, weary of the Shadow Council's deceit, started to rally. A grassroots

movement, The Dawn Brigade,'
emerged, dedicated to restoring the
planet's ecosystems and rebuilding the
foundations of society.

The Final Stand

In a decisive battle for Earth's future,
the Dawn Brigade, supported by the
Guardians and the Star Sentinels,
confronted the Shadow Council. The
industrialists' stronghold was besieged,
and their schemes unraveled one by one.

The Reclamation of Earth

With the fall of the Shadow Council,
Earth began the arduous journey of
healing. The Dawn Brigade led the
efforts to redistribute resources, restore
the damaged ecosystems, and rekindle
the spirit of cooperation that had once
defined the planet.

Epilogue: The Resilience of Hope

The Shadow Council's attempt to seize control had ultimately failed, but not without cost. Earth had endured a great trial, yet the resilience of its people shone through the darkness. The Age of Harmony was not just preserved; it was strengthened and tempered by the fires of adversity and humanity's unyielding hope.

The Shadow Council's gambit had shaken the core of Earth's society, revealing the vulnerabilities beneath the surface of the Age of Harmony. The industrial magnates, blinded by their thirst for power, had underestimated the people's collective will.

The Awakening of the Masses

Once divided, the masses awakened to the reality of their situation. The seeds of sedition planted by the Shadow

Council sprouted into a unifying force as communities banded together to protect their homes and planet.

The Guardians' Resolve

The Guardians of Harmony, faced with the internal strife on Earth, found new resolve in their mission. They worked in the shadows, supporting the Dawn Brigade and the loyal forces of Earth to restore order and peace.

The Silent Sentinels' Strategy

The Silent Sentinels, the covert arm of the United Galaxies Council, employed a strategy of precision and stealth. They infiltrated the Shadow Council's networks, exposing their conspiracies and cutting off their avenues of influence.

The Dawn Brigade's Rise

The Dawn Brigade, a mosaic of Earth's bravest souls, rose from the ashes of conflict. They became the symbol of Earth's indomitable spirit, leading the charge to reclaim their planet from the brink of collapse.

The Battle for Earth's Soul

The final stand against the Shadow Council was more than a physical confrontation; it was a battle for Earth's soul. The industrialists' fortress, once impregnable, fell to the united front of the Dawn Brigade and their allies.

The Rebirth of a Planet

The reclamation of Earth was a testament to the resilience of its ecosystems and its people. Once on the verge of ecological and societal collapse, the planet began to heal under the careful stewardship of the Dawn Brigade.

The Resilience of Hope

The epilogue of this dark chapter in Earth's history was written with the ink of hope. The trials faced by humanity had forged a stronger, more united civilization, ready to face the future with renewed vigor and wisdom.

The chapter concludes with Earth emerging from the shadow of the Council's gambit, not weakened but fortified. The Age of Harmony, once threatened, now stood as a beacon of hope for all civilizations that looked upon Earth as a shining example of what could be achieved when unity triumphs over division.

Chapter 25: The UGC Assistance to Earth

In the wake of global upheaval, the United Galaxies Council (UGC) initiated a comprehensive assistance program to support Earth's recovery. This multifaceted approach aimed not only to rebuild but to revolutionize Earth's infrastructure, integrating cutting-edge technologies to foster a sustainable future.

Reconstruction of Infrastructure

The UGC's financial aid targeted the reconstruction of essential services and facilities. Educational institutions were redesigned to foster innovation and critical thinking, while healthcare facilities were equipped with advanced medical technologies to improve patient care. Public utilities were overhauled to become models of efficiency and sustainability.

Advanced Environmental Technologies

To enhance Earth's environmental management, the UGC introduced several advanced technologies:

- *Artificial Intelligence (AI):* AI systems optimize resource distribution, manage waste, and monitor environmental health, adapting in real-time to the planet's needs.
- *Blockchain:* This technology ensured transparency and security in resource usage and environmental data, creating an immutable ledger that promoted accountability.
- *Big Data Analytics:* By analyzing vast amounts of environmental data, big data tools provide insights to predict trends, prevent

disasters, and facilitate efficient resource management.

- *Internet of Things (IoT):* IoT devices deployed across various ecosystems collect real-time data, which informs sustainable practices and environmental stewardship.

Sustainability Technologies

The UGC identified several sustainability technologies poised for widespread adoption:

- *Cloud Sustainability:* Centralizing IT operations through cloud services led to greater computing efficiency and a significant reduction in carbon footprint.
- *Carbon Footprint Measurement:* New technologies emerged to measure and manage the carbon footprint of products and services, covering all emission scopes.

- *Advanced Grid Management Software:* This software enhanced the efficiency of power grids, seamlessly integrating renewable energy sources and improving electricity distribution.

Enhancing Efficiency in Environmental Services

The integration of these technologies transformed Earth's environmental services, leading to significant enhancements in efficiency and sustainability. Automated processes, real-time monitoring, and predictive analytics revolutionized environmental stewardship, reducing waste and optimizing operational workflows.

The Path Forward

With the UGC's assistance, Earth embarked on a path of recovery and renewal. The advanced technologies provided by the UGC not only helped manage the immediate crisis but also laid the groundwork for a sustainable future. Earth's citizens, now equipped with the tools and knowledge to manage their planet responsibly, looked forward to a new era of prosperity and environmental harmony.

The UGC's intervention was a turning point for Earth. The council's vision extended beyond mere reconstruction; it sought to empower Earth's citizens to become active stewards of their homes. The technologies introduced were not just solutions to current problems but investments in Earth's future.

The Cultural Renaissance

Alongside infrastructure and technology, the UGC recognized the importance of cultural revitalization. Programs were established to celebrate Earth's diverse heritage, fostering a sense of global community and shared responsibility for the planet's future.

The Economic Revival

Economic initiatives were launched to stimulate growth and provide opportunities in the new green economy. These initiatives supported the development of sustainable businesses and promoted green jobs, aligning economic prosperity with environmental responsibility.

The Educational Revolution

Educational reforms were implemented to prepare the next generation for the challenges of a sustainable future. Curricula were updated to include environmental science, sustainability, and space studies, ensuring that students were equipped with the knowledge and skills to thrive in the Age of Harmony.

The Health of the Planet

The UGC's environmental technologies played a crucial role in restoring Earth's natural ecosystems. Programs were launched to clean the oceans, reforest the land, and purify the air, healing the planet from the scars of the past.

The Legacy of Assistance

The legacy of the UGC's assistance to Earth was one of transformation and hope. The council's support had not only helped Earth recover from the crisis but had also set it on a course towards a brighter, more sustainable future.

Epilogue: A New Dawn

As the Earth healed and grew under the UGC's guidance, a new dawn broke on the horizon. The planet, once on the brink of ecological collapse, now stood as a shining example of what could be achieved when the wisdom of the stars was combined with the resolve of humanity.

Chapter 26: A Decade of Renaissance

A decade had unfolded since the pivotal moment when the United Galaxies Council (UGC) extended its benevolent hand to Earth. The planet, teetering on the precipice of ecological and societal collapse, has since been transformed into a paragon of sustainability and unity. This renaissance has reshaped the very fabric of human civilization.

Social Renaissance

From the ashes of the old world, society has been reborn. The UGC's advanced technologies catalyzed an era of social responsibility and community engagement. Once bastions of rote learning, educational institutions have flourished into vibrant hubs of innovation and cultural exchange. These learning centers have become crucibles for developing new ideas and fostering a generation of thinkers, creators, and leaders equipped to navigate the complexities of a rapidly evolving galaxy.

Healthcare systems, previously beleaguered by inefficiency and inaccessibility, have undergone a revolution. Universal access to health services is now a reality, ensuring that every citizen is afforded the care and support needed to lead a healthy and productive life. The integration of AI diagnostics, telemedicine, and personalized treatments has not only extended lifespans but also enhanced the quality of life, allowing individuals to contribute meaningfully to their communities.

Economic Revival

The economic landscape of Earth has witnessed a seismic shift. The introduction of UGC technologies has spurred a green industrial revolution, creating a surge in sustainable industries. Millions of jobs have been generated, each contributing to the preservation of Earth's delicate ecosystems. The adoption of blockchain and AI-driven economies has ushered in an era of transparency and efficiency, virtually eliminating corruption and waste. This economic revival has been inclusive, lifting millions out of poverty and providing opportunities for all, regardless of background or social standing.

Happiness and Well-Being

The happiness quotient among Earth's citizens has reached unprecedented levels. The World Happiness Report, a barometer of global well-being, now ranks Earth among the top contenders—a remarkable ascent from its modest placement a decade prior. The sense of community, security, and optimism that permeates the air is tangible. People have not only adapted to the new technologies but have wholeheartedly embraced the cultural paradigm shift towards sustainability and unity.

The Final Conclusion

As this chapter of Earth's story draws to a close, we reflect on the odyssey that has led to this moment. The planet, once on the brink of annihilation, now stands as a testament to the extraordinary feats that can be achieved when unity and technology converge for the greater good. The Shadow Council's divisive attempts are now a distant memory, serving as a stark reminder of the paths not taken and the perils of power unchecked.

The Dawn Brigade, the unsung heroes of this tale, continue their silent vigil. They are the custodians of Earth's future, a future that shines brightly with promise and potential. Their tireless efforts ensure that past lessons remain at the forefront of collective consciousness, guiding decisions and shaping a resilient, harmonious, and forward-looking world.

In the end, Earth's narrative is one of hope, resilience, and the indomitable spirit of humanity. It is a saga that will echo through the annals of time, a chronicle of a world reborn from the clutches of despair, a world united in purpose, and a world that has found its place in the harmonious chorus of the stars.

And so, we conclude this epic journey with Earth not merely surviving but thriving—a beacon of prosperity and peace, a luminary in the vast cosmos, and a sanctuary to contented souls living in a society that epitomizes progress and joy. The Decade of the Renaissance has been a golden age for Earth, setting the stage for centuries of prosperity and interstellar camaraderie.

But before we come to the last page of this odyssey, let us raise some questions and try to answer them. Here we go:

☐ How did Earth react to this cosmic intervention?

Earth's reaction to cosmic intervention was profound and transformative. Initially marked by skepticism and fear, the intervention soon proved to be a catalyst for unparalleled progress and unity. The introduction of UGC technologies sparked a green industrial revolution, fostering sustainable industries and creating millions of jobs dedicated to preserving Earth's ecosystems. Blockchain and AI-driven economies revolutionized transparency and efficiency, almost completely eradicating corruption and waste.

This technological and economic renaissance was inclusive, lifting millions out of poverty and providing equal opportunities for all citizens. The societal shift towards sustainability and unity was widely embraced, fostering a sense of community, security, and optimism. Earth's happiness quotient soared, as evidenced by its top ranking in the World Happiness Report—a significant leap from its previous standing a decade earlier.

The intervention also served as a unifying force against previously divisive elements, such as the Shadow Council. The collective efforts of the Dawn Brigade, Earth's guardians of the future, ensured that the lessons of the past remained at the forefront of global consciousness, driving decisions toward a resilient and harmonious world. Overall, Earth's response was one of hope, resilience, and a commitment to a prosperous future.

☐ Are there any rivalries or conflicts within the council?

Despite the transformative and unifying impact of the cosmic intervention on Earth, rivalries and conflicts within the council persisted. These disputes often emerged from differing priorities and philosophies among member civilizations, each with unique cultural and historical backgrounds. The council, comprising many diverse societies, faced challenges in balancing the need for progress with the preservation of individual identities.

The Shadow Council, a divisive element highlighted in Earth's story, reminds us of the persistent undercurrents of conflict. Their attempts to disrupt unity underscore the inherent complexities of governing a diverse galaxy. However, the council's commitment to transparency and efficiency, bolstered by UGC technologies such as blockchain and AI, played a crucial role in mitigating these conflicts.

The Dawn Brigade's vigilant efforts ensured that lessons from past rivalries remained central to decision-making processes. This proactive approach fostered a resilient and harmonious world, demonstrating that conflicts, though inevitable, could be managed effectively through collective effort and progressive policies. In summary, while rivalries and disputes within the council exist, they are countered by mechanisms and guardians dedicated to upholding unity and fostering a prosperous future.

☐ How does the UGC handle disputes between member civilizations?

The UGC handles disputes between member civilizations with a multifaceted approach rooted in transparency, efficiency, and inclusivity. Utilizing advanced technologies such as blockchain and AI, the council ensures that all conflicts are addressed with utmost integrity and clarity. These technologies provide a transparent framework for decision-making, thus minimizing the risk of corruption and bias.

The council fosters open dialogue and mutual understanding among civilizations, recognizing the unique cultural and historical backgrounds that each member brings to the table. This inclusive approach emphasizes the preservation of individual identities while striving for collective progress. Regular forums and assemblies are held where representatives can voice their concerns and negotiate solutions.

Furthermore, the vigilant efforts of the Dawn Brigade play a crucial role in mediating disputes. As guardians of the future, they ensure that lessons from past rivalries remain central to decision-making processes. This proactive stance helps manage conflicts effectively, fostering resilience and harmony within the council.

While disputes are inevitable, the UGC's commitment to progressive policies and collective effort enables it to handle them efficiently, aiming to uphold unity and a prosperous future for all member civilizations.

☐ What role do trade, and commerce play within the council?

Trade and commerce within the council serve as vital instruments for fostering unity and collaboration among member civilizations. The diverse cultural and historical backgrounds of each civilization necessitate an inclusive approach, emphasizing mutual benefit and collective progress. The council employs advanced technologies, such as blockchain and AI, to ensure transparency and efficiency in commercial transactions, thereby minimizing the risks of corruption and bias.

The exchange of goods, services, and knowledge across civilizations not only boosts economies but also strengthens diplomatic relations. Regular forums and assemblies provide platforms for representatives to negotiate trade agreements and resolve economic disputes. Furthermore, trade serves as a conduit for cultural exchange, allowing civilizations to share their unique identities while contributing to the council's collective prosperity.

The Dawn Brigade plays a crucial role in overseeing trade activities, ensuring that lessons from past commercial rivalries inform current policies. This vigilant approach helps maintain a balanced and equitable economic environment within the council.

In summary, trade and commerce are essential components of the council's framework, driving economic growth, fostering diplomatic relations, and enhancing cultural exchange, all while upholding the principles of transparency and inclusivity.

☐ *Are there any rogue factions or outliers in the galaxy that challenge the UGC's ideals?*

Although the narrative does not explicitly mention rogue factions or outliers challenging the UGC's ideals, it can be inferred that the existence of such entities is plausible given the complex dynamics of inter-civilizational relations. The UGC's multifaceted approach to dispute resolution, incorporating advanced technologies like blockchain and AI, suggests that maintaining integrity and clarity in decision-making is paramount. This mechanism would be essential in addressing challenges posed by any factions that diverge from the council's principles.

The Dawn Brigade's proactive stance, which mediates disputes and ensures the incorporation of lessons from past rivalries, highlights the council's awareness of potential threats to its unity. This brigade's vigilant efforts are indicative of a system designed to counteract any internal or external forces that may undermine the collective progress and harmony of member civilizations.

Overall, while rogue factions or outliers are not explicitly discussed, the narrative implies that the UGC is equipped to handle such challenges through its robust, transparent, and inclusive mechanisms. The emphasis on mutual understanding, resilience, and progressive policies further supports the council's capacity to uphold its ideals against any opposition.

☐ *Are there any intergalactic sports or competitions?*

Intergalactic sports and competitions are integral to the cultural fabric of the Universal Galactic Council (UGC). These events serve as a platform for member civilizations to showcase their prowess, foster unity, and celebrate diversity. The council organizes annual games that feature a wide array of disciplines, ranging from traditional physical sports to advanced technological challenges and intellectual contests. These competitions not only promote physical fitness and mental agility but also encourage collaboration and mutual respect among participants from different civilizations.

The sports events are meticulously planned to ensure inclusivity and fairness, with advanced technologies like AI and blockchain used to monitor and adjudicate performances. These technologies help maintain transparency and minimize disputes, reflecting the council's commitment to integrity.

Moreover, intergalactic competitions facilitate cultural exchange, allowing civilizations to share their unique traditions and innovations. Spectators from across the galaxy gather to witness the remarkable displays of skill and ingenuity, reinforcing the sense of community within the UGC. In essence, these sports and competitions are more than just entertainment; they are a vital tool for fostering unity, celebrating diversity, and upholding the council's ideals.

☐ What role do art and literature play in this galactic society? ☐ Are there any historical examples of cultural conflicts within the UGC?

Art and literature play a pivotal role in the galactic society of the Universal Galactic Council (UGC), serving as essential mediums for cultural expression and unity. These creative forms foster a shared understanding and respect among the diverse member civilizations. Art and literature are used to communicate history, values, and perspectives, thereby bridging cultural gaps and promoting mutual appreciation. Through various artistic and literary endeavors, civilizations can showcase their unique heritage, contributing to a richer, more cohesive community.

Regarding historical examples of cultural conflicts within the UGC, the narrative does not explicitly detail specific instances. However, it hints at the existence of such conflicts given the council's elaborate mechanisms for dispute resolution and the proactive efforts of the Dawn Brigade. The brigade's role in mediating disputes and incorporating lessons from past rivalries underscores the UGC's awareness of potential cultural tensions. This vigilant approach ensures that any cultural conflicts are addressed promptly, maintaining the unity and harmony of the council. Overall, the focus on transparency, inclusivity, and advanced technologies in decision-making suggests a robust framework to manage and resolve cultural disputes within the UGC.

☐ Are there any historical conflicts over rare or unique resources?

While the narrative does not explicitly detail specific historical conflicts over rare or unique resources within the Universal Galactic Council (UGC), it implies the existence of such tensions. The council's comprehensive mechanisms for dispute resolution and the proactive stance of the Dawn Brigade suggest that resource conflicts have occurred and have been managed effectively. The UGC's emphasis on mutual understanding, resilience, and progressive policies supports its capacity to handle disputes over valuable resources. These potential conflicts are addressed through transparent, inclusive processes and advanced technologies, ensuring fairness and minimizing disputes. Thus, while rare resource conflicts are not explicitly mentioned, the structure of the UGC indicates a robust framework for managing such challenges and maintaining the unity and harmony of its member civilizations.

☐ What role does scientific research play in resource allocation decisions within the UGC?

Scientific research plays a crucial role in resource allocation decisions within the Universal Galactic Council (UGC). The council relies on advanced scientific methodologies to assess the availability, sustainability, and equitable distribution of resources across its member civilizations. These decisions are informed by rigorous data analysis, environmental impact studies, and technological evaluations, ensuring that the allocation is both efficient and fair.

Research findings guide the UGC in prioritizing resource needs, identifying potential shortages, and developing innovative solutions to address them. By leveraging scientific insights, the council can anticipate future demands and implement measures to mitigate conflicts over scarce resources. Furthermore, the integration of scientific research into resource management promotes transparency and fosters trust among member civilizations, as decisions are based on objective evidence rather than political motives.

In essence, scientific research underpins the UGC's resource allocation strategies, ensuring that they are sustainable, equitable, and aligned with the council's commitment to unity and harmony. Through continual advancements in research, the UGC is able to adapt to changing circumstances, uphold its ideals, and maintain the stability of its galactic society.

☐ *Have there been any historical conflicts that threatened the stability of the UGC?*

While the Universal Galactic Council's (UGC) narrative does not delve into specific historical conflicts that have threatened its stability, it is evident that such challenges have existed. The elaborate dispute-resolution mechanisms and the Dawn Brigade's proactive efforts indicate that the UGC has faced and managed significant conflicts. These conflicts likely stem from cultural differences, resource allocation disputes, and technological advancements.

The Dawn Brigade's role in mediating disputes and incorporating lessons from past rivalries underscores the UGC's awareness and preparedness for potential threats to stability. The council's focus on transparency, inclusivity, and advanced technologies in decision-making suggests a robust framework to manage and resolve conflicts. This vigilant approach ensures that any threats to stability are addressed promptly, maintaining unity and harmony within the council.

While the narrative does not explicitly detail any specific historical conflicts, the UGC's structure and strategies imply that it has successfully navigated various challenges. The emphasis on mutual understanding, resilience, and progressive policies supports the UGC's capacity to uphold its ideals and maintain the stability of its galactic society.

☐ *What role does scientific research play in resolving inter-civilizational conflicts within the UGC?*

Scientific research plays a pivotal role in resolving inter-civilizational conflicts within the Universal Galactic Council (UGC). By leveraging advanced scientific methodologies, the UGC can analyze and address the root causes of conflicts with objectivity and precision. This includes conducting thorough environmental impact studies, sociocultural assessments, and technological evaluations to understand the implications of various disputes.

Research findings inform the council's decision-making processes, ensuring that solutions are grounded in empirical evidence rather than political bias. This approach promotes transparency and fosters trust among member civilizations, as scientific insights provide a neutral basis for negotiations and resolutions. Furthermore, the integration of research into conflict resolution enables the UGC to anticipate future tensions and develop proactive measures to mitigate them.

By continuously advancing scientific knowledge, the UGC is able to adapt its strategies to the evolving needs and dynamics of its galactic society. This commitment to research ensures that the council's actions align with its ideals of unity and harmony, ultimately maintaining stability and fostering peaceful coexistence among diverse civilizations. In essence, scientific research underpins the UGC's efforts to resolve conflicts, making them sustainable, equitable, and effective.

☐ *Can we provide an example of a specific cultural clash within the UGC?*

We can illustrate a hypothetical example of a cultural clash within the Universal Galactic Council (UGC). Imagine a scenario where the resource-rich planet of Zorath, inhabited by a civilization that prioritizes spiritual rituals involving extensive land use, is at odds with the neighboring technologically advanced civilization of Arcturia. The Arcturians propose the construction of a spaceport on Zorath to facilitate interplanetary trade and technological exchange, which they argue would benefit all member civilizations.

However, the Zorathians view the proposal as a direct threat to their sacred lands, integral to their cultural identity and spiritual practices. Their objection stems from the belief that the technological infrastructure would disrupt the harmony and sanctity of their rituals, leading to cultural erosion.

The UGC intervenes by leveraging scientific research to assess the impact of the proposed spaceport on Zorath's environment and cultural heritage. Mediation efforts led by the Dawn Brigade result in a compromise: the spaceport will be constructed in a manner that preserves the sacred sites, with advanced technology ensuring minimal environmental disruption. This resolution underscores the UGC's commitment to balancing technological advancement with cultural preservation, fostering unity amid diversity.

☐ *What role do art and literature play in bridging cultural gaps within the UGC?*

Art and literature serve as powerful tools for bridging cultural gaps within the Universal Galactic Council (UGC). Artistic expressions and literary works transcend linguistic and cultural barriers, offering a universal language through which civilizations can share their unique experiences, values, and traditions. Through art, member civilizations can visually communicate their heritage and ideals, fostering a deeper appreciation and understanding among diverse cultures.

Literature, on the other hand, provides narratives that explore the complexities of different societies, allowing readers to immerse themselves in the lives and perspectives of others. This narrative immersion cultivates empathy and respect, which are essential components for harmonious coexistence. By hosting intergalactic art exhibitions, literary festivals, and cultural exchanges, the UGC creates platforms for dialogue and collaboration where civilizations can celebrate their diversity while finding common ground.

Furthermore, art and literature often address universal themes such as love, conflict, and identity, highlighting shared human experiences that resonate across galaxies. These creative forms inspire conversations and reflections that pave the way for mutual respect and unity. In essence, art and literature are the heartbeats of the UGC, pulsing with creativity and connection, bridging the vast expanse of cultural differences.

□ How do civilizations handle disputes when their spiritual practices clash with technological infrastructure or space exploration plans?

When civilizations within the Universal Galactic Council (UGC) encounter disputes where spiritual practices clash with technological infrastructure or space exploration plans, the council employs a multifaceted approach to mediation and resolution. Firstly, comprehensive scientific research is conducted to understand the potential impacts of proposed technological projects on spiritual and cultural sites. This research helps in making informed decisions that balance development with cultural preservation.

The UGC also facilitates dialogue between the conflicting parties, fostering an environment where each civilization can express its concerns and priorities. Mediation is often led by specialized teams, such as the Dawn Brigade, who work to find compromises that respect both technological aspirations and spiritual traditions. Solutions might include modifying infrastructure plans to avoid sacred areas, implementing advanced technologies that minimize environmental disruption, or establishing buffer zones that protect cultural heritage.

In addition, the UGC promotes the integration of cultural experts and spiritual leaders into the planning process, ensuring that development projects are designed with sensitivity to cultural values. By prioritizing mutual respect and understanding, the UGC aims to achieve sustainable resolutions that honor its member civilizations' diverse identities and traditions.

☐ *What role does philosophy play in bridging gaps between religion and science within the UGC?*

Philosophy plays a pivotal role in bridging gaps between religion and science within the Universal Galactic Council (UGC) by providing a framework for dialogue and understanding. It encourages civilizations to explore fundamental questions about existence, ethics, and the universe, fostering a shared quest for knowledge that transcends disciplinary boundaries.

Religion often offers insights into spiritual and moral dimensions of life, while science seeks to understand the material and empirical aspects. Philosophy acts as a mediator, exploring concepts like truth, reality, and the nature of being, which are relevant to both domains. By emphasizing critical thinking and the examination of underlying principles, philosophy helps reconcile religious beliefs with scientific discoveries, promoting a harmonious coexistence.

Furthermore, philosophy encourages the integration of diverse perspectives, advocating for an inclusive approach that respects both spiritual traditions and scientific methodologies. It facilitates discussions on ethical implications of technological advancements and the preservation of cultural heritage, ensuring that decisions reflect a balance between progress and reverence for spiritual values.

Through philosophical inquiry, the UGC cultivates a culture of mutual respect and intellectual collaboration, paving the way for unified efforts in addressing complex challenges and advancing collective understanding.

☐ *What other conflicts have arisen due to technological advancements within the UGC?*

Other conflicts that have arisen due to technological advancements within the Universal Galactic Council (UGC) include issues related to artificial intelligence (AI) and automation. Some civilizations have faced ethical dilemmas regarding the use of AI in decision-making processes, fearing that it may undermine traditional leadership roles and cultural practices. Concerns about privacy and surveillance have also emerged, with advanced technologies enabling unprecedented data collection and monitoring capabilities. These advancements can lead to tensions between those advocating for security and efficiency versus those prioritizing personal freedoms and privacy.

Moreover, the development of powerful energy sources like antimatter and fusion has sparked disputes over resource allocation and environmental risks. Civilizations worry about the potential for catastrophic accidents and the exploitation of these technologies for destructive purposes. The UGC addresses such conflicts by ensuring stringent regulations and promoting transparent dialogue among member civilizations.

Lastly, the introduction of genetic engineering and bio-enhancement technologies raises moral questions about human and species identity, equity, and ethical boundaries. The UGC strives to balance innovation with ethical considerations, fostering an inclusive approach that respects its members' diverse values and beliefs.

☐ Are there any factions or radical groups that reject such compromises in favor of absolute adherence to the UGC's primary goals?

Indeed, within the diverse expanse of the Universal Galactic Council (UGC), there exist factions that vehemently oppose compromises and advocate for stringent adherence to the UGC's primary goals. These groups, often composed of idealists and radicals, believe that any deviation from the council's foundational principles undermines the integrity and future of the coalition. They argue that compromises dilute the UGC's objectives, leading to moral and ethical ambiguity.

Such factions often reject advances in artificial intelligence, genetic engineering, and other technologies that pose risks to traditional values and the essence of various species. They also resist policies that are too lenient on environmental stewardship and cultural preservation. By promoting a purist approach, these groups seek to maintain the original vision of the UGC, even if it means opposing more progressive or integrative measures proposed by other member civilizations.

While their stance can create tensions within the UGC, it also serves as a reminder of the diverse perspectives that shape the council's deliberations and ensure that all voices are heard in the quest for a harmonious galactic society.

After we have answered the questions that were raised in our minds by this Odessey, let us explore the Galaxy world further.

The United Galaxies Council (UGC), while a fictional entity in our creative narrative, is envisioned to have primary goals that reflect the collective aspirations of its member civilizations. These goals would likely include:

- *Peaceful Coexistence:* Promoting harmony and preventing conflicts among the diverse civilizations within the Milky Way galaxy.
- *Sustainable Development:* Ensuring that all member civilizations can grow and prosper without depleting the natural resources of their planets and the galaxy at large.
- *Scientific Advancement:* Facilitating the sharing of knowledge and

technology to further scientific understanding and innovation.

- *Cultural Exchange:* Encouraging the exchange of cultural practices and philosophies to enrich the lives of all galactic citizens.
- *Environmental Stewardship:* Protecting the ecological balance of planets and addressing issues like space debris and planetary pollution.
- *Exploration and Discovery:* Supporting missions and research that expand the frontiers of knowledge about the universe.

These goals would be pursued to create a sustainable and thriving galactic society where the welfare of each planet and species is considered in the context of the greater good of the galaxy. The UGC would likely operate under a charter that emphasizes collaboration, respect for autonomy and shared responsibility for the well-being of the cosmic community.

The United Galaxies Civilizations

The United Galaxies Council (UGC) is a vast and diverse coalition encompassing a wide array of civilizations, each with its unique attributes and contributions to the council. Here's a glimpse into some of the member civilizations:

- *The Andorians:* Known for their blue skin and antennae, the Andorians are a highly disciplined and valiant militaristic race. They hail from the icy world of Andoria and are founding members of the UGC. Their contributions to defense and security are invaluable.
- The Vulcans: Originating from the planet Vulcan, they are a logical and non-emotional species that prioritize the pursuit of knowledge. Their advanced

technologies and commitment to peace and diplomacy play a pivotal role in the UGC's operations.

- *The Tellarites:* These argumentative and industrious beings come from Tellar. They are known for their debating skills and contribute to the UGC with their diplomatic prowess and trade negotiations.
- *The Betazoids:* With their telepathic abilities, the Betazoids from Betazed offer unique insights into communication and conflict resolution, aiding the UGC in maintaining harmony among its members.
- The Trill: A joined species with a symbiotic relationship between a humanoid host and a symbiont, the Trill comes from the planet. They bring a wealth of experience and memories from past hosts,

enriching the cultural and historical knowledge of the UGC.

* *The Bajorans:* Spiritual and resilient, the Bajorans from Bajor have endured much suffering. Their spiritual insights and artistic contributions add depth to the UGC's cultural tapestry.

These are just a few examples of the civilizations that form the backbone of the UGC. Each member brings their strengths, creating a collective that is robust, enlightened, and dedicated to the welfare of the Milky Way galaxy. The UGC's mission is to ensure that all civilizations can coexist peacefully, share resources, and work together for the common good of the galaxy.

How do these civilizations interact with each other?

The civilizations within the United Galaxies Council (UGC) interact with each other through a complex web of diplomatic, cultural, and scientific exchanges, fostering a vibrant intergalactic community. Here's how they might interact:

- *Diplomatic Relations:* Civilizations engage in formal diplomatic activities, including treaties, alliances, and trade agreements. The UGC serves as a neutral platform for resolving disputes and negotiating peace.
- *Cultural Festivals:* Intergalactic cultural festivals are common, where civilizations showcase their arts, music, and traditions. These events are crucial for building mutual respect and understanding.
- *Scientific Collaborations:* Joint research initiatives and shared space missions allow civilizations to pool their knowledge and resources to advance science and exploration.

- *Educational Exchanges:* Students and scholars from different worlds participate in exchange programs, studying abroad to learn new perspectives and skills.
- *Interspecies Communication:* With various communication methods, from verbal to telepathic, civilizations have developed universal translators and protocols to facilitate clear and respectful dialogue.
- *Trade and Commerce:* A galactic market thrives with the exchange of goods, services, and technologies. Trade routes crisscross the Milky Way, managed by the UGC, to ensure fair and ethical commerce.
- *Emergency Aid:* In times of crisis, such as natural disasters or pandemics, civilizations come together to provide assistance and support to the affected world.

Through these interactions, the UGC aims to create a cohesive and cooperative galaxy where diversity is celebrated and collective challenges are met with unity and innovation. The council ensures that these interactions are governed by principles of equality, non-interference, and mutual benefit, securing a prosperous future for all its members.

How do civilizations handle cultural misunderstandings or conflicts?

In the context of the United Galaxies Council (UGC), civilizations would handle cultural misunderstandings or conflicts through a variety of mechanisms designed to foster understanding, respect, and peaceful resolution. Here's how they might approach such challenges:

- *Intercultural Education:* Civilizations invest in education programs that teach about the customs, communication styles, and social norms of different cultures within the UGC. This helps prevent misunderstandings and stereotypes.

- *Conflict Resolution Committees:* Specialized committees or mediators with expertise in intercultural relations are established to address and resolve conflicts. They work to understand the root causes and facilitate dialogue between parties.
- *Cultural Liaisons:* Each civilization appoints cultural liaisons who are well-versed in the customs of other member civilizations. These individuals act as bridges, helping to navigate and resolve cultural misunderstandings.
- *Universal Protocols:* The UGC develops universal protocols for communication and interaction

that all member civilizations agree to follow, reducing the likelihood of misunderstandings.

- *Empathy Training:* Members of the UGC undergo training to develop empathy and the ability to view situations from the perspective of other cultures, which is crucial for resolving conflicts.
- *Joint Cultural Celebrations:* Regularly scheduled events where different civilizations celebrate their heritage together encourage mutual respect and understanding.
- *Restorative Justice Practices:* When conflicts do arise, the UGC favors restorative justice practices that focus on healing and reconciliation rather than punishment.
- *Intergalactic Exchange Programs:* Exchange programs for citizens of different civilizations, including students, artists, and

professionals, promote firsthand understanding of different cultures.

These strategies help ensure that any cultural misunderstandings or conflicts within the UGC are handled with a focus on unity, respect, and the shared goal of maintaining a harmonious intergalactic community. The UGC's approach is likely to be proactive, emphasizing prevention and education while also equipping it to address issues as they arise with sensitivity and a commitment to peaceful resolution.

How do civilizations handle disputes related to resource allocation or territorial claims?

In the United Galaxies Council (UGC) narrative, disputes related to resource allocation or territorial claims would be handled through a structured and diplomatic process guided by principles of fairness, sustainability, and mutual respect. Here's how such disputes might be addressed:

- *Mediation and Arbitration:* The UGC would likely have a system in place for mediation and arbitration, where neutral parties help to facilitate discussions and propose solutions that are acceptable to all involved parties.

- *Intergalactic Legal Framework:* There would be a comprehensive legal framework that outlines the rights and responsibilities of civilizations regarding resource use and territorial boundaries. This framework would be used as a basis for resolving disputes.

- *Resource Sharing Agreements:* Civilizations might enter into agreements that outline the terms for sharing resources, ensuring that all civilizations have access to what they need while protecting the interests of those who hold the resources.

- *Territorial Negotiations:* When it comes to territorial claims, negotiations would be conducted to reach a mutually beneficial arrangement, possibly involving exchanges of territory or resources.
- *Economic Compensation:* In some cases, economic compensation might be offered to resolve disputes, with one civilization providing financial or resource-based compensation to another.
- *Intergalactic Court:* There could be an intergalactic court where disputes can be formally adjudicated based on evidence and legal principles.
- *Consensus Building:* The UGC would encourage consensus building through dialogue and understanding, aiming for solutions that are agreed upon by all parties.

- *Preventive Diplomacy:* Proactive diplomacy and the establishment of clear guidelines for resource extraction and territorial exploration would be used to prevent disputes from arising.

These mechanisms would be designed to ensure that disputes are resolved in a way that maintains the galaxy's stability and the well-being of all its inhabitants. The UGC's approach would emphasize peaceful resolution and the avoidance of conflict, reflecting the council's overarching goals of peaceful coexistence and sustainable development.

How do civilizations handle disputes when their interests directly conflict with each other?

In the scenario of the United Galaxies Council (UGC), when member civilizations have interests that directly conflict with each other, they would likely employ a combination of advanced conflict resolution methods to navigate these disputes. Here's how they might handle such situations:

- *Diplomatic Negotiations:* Civilizations engage in high-level diplomatic talks to find common ground and work towards mutually beneficial solutions.
- *Conflict Resolution Panels:* Panels composed of representatives from neutral civilizations could be formed to hear all sides of the dispute and offer fair, unbiased recommendations.
- *Intergalactic Mediators:* Trained mediators who understand the cultures and values of the conflicting parties would facilitate discussions to help them reach an agreement.
- *Binding Arbitration:* In cases where negotiations fail, the parties may agree to binding

arbitration, where a neutral
arbitrator makes a decision that
all parties agree to abide by.

- *Resource Redistribution:* The UGC
  might oversee a redistribution of
  resources or territories to ensure
  that all civilizations' needs are
  met without compromising
  others' interests.
- *Economic Sanctions or Incentives:*
  The UGC could impose sanctions
  on a civilization that refuses to
  negotiate or offer incentives for
  those that agree to compromise.
- *Intergalactic Law Enforcement:* If a
  civilization acts against the
  UGC's collective agreements, law
  enforcement mechanisms could be
  in place to address such
  violations.
- *Peacekeeping Forces:* The UGC
  might deploy peacekeeping forces
  to maintain order and prevent
  conflicts from escalating into
  warfare.

- *Public Diplomacy:* Civilizations might engage in public diplomacy, appealing to the citizens of the conflicting civilizations to build support for peaceful resolution.
- *Intergalactic Court System:* A court system with jurisdiction over intergalactic disputes could adjudicate conflicts and issue rulings based on a shared legal framework.

These methods would be underpinned by the UGC's commitment to peaceful coexistence, respect for sovereignty, and the well-being of the galaxy. The council would strive to ensure that all disputes are resolved in a manner that upholds the principles of justice and equity while also preserving the unity and stability of the intergalactic community.

How do civilizations handle disputes when cultural values clash with practical interests?

When cultural values clash with practical interests within the United Galaxies Council (UGC), the civilizations would likely employ a multifaceted approach to reconcile these differences and find a resolution. Here's how they might handle such disputes:

- *Cultural Sensitivity Training:* Civilizations engage in training to understand and respect the cultural values of others, which helps prevent conflicts and foster empathy.
- *Value-Based Mediation:* Mediators skilled in navigating cultural nuances would facilitate discussions, focusing on the underlying values and beliefs to find common ground.
- *Ethical Frameworks:* The UGC would have ethical frameworks that balance cultural values with practical needs, guiding

civilizations in making decisions that honor both aspects.

- *Dialogue and Communication:* Open and honest communication channels would be established to discuss the implications of cultural values and practical interests, aiming for transparency and understanding.
- *Compromise and Adaptation:* Civilizations would be encouraged to compromise and adapt their practices where possible to accommodate others' cultural values while still meeting practical needs.
- *Policy Development:* The UGC would develop policies that consider the diversity of cultural values and the practical realities of resource allocation, technology use, and other interests.
- *Intercultural Advisory Panels:* Panels consisting of representatives from various

cultures would provide insights
and advice on how to manage
disputes that involve cultural
values and practical interests.

- *Shared Vision and Goals:* By
  focusing on shared visions and
  overarching goals, civilizations
  can often find ways to align their
  cultural values with practical
  interests for the greater good.

These strategies would be underpinned
by the UGC's commitment to peaceful
coexistence and the well-being of the
galaxy, ensuring that disputes are
resolved in a manner that respects
cultural diversity and effectively
addresses practical concerns.

*How do civilizations handle disputes when
their religious beliefs conflict with scientific
advancements or technological practices?*

In a scenario where the United Galaxies
Council (UGC) is faced with disputes

arising from conflicts between religious beliefs and scientific advancements or technological practices, the civilizations would likely approach the situation with a combination of respect for diversity and a commitment to progress. Here's how they might handle such disputes:

- *Dialogue and Understanding:* Civilizations would engage in open dialogue to understand the perspectives and concerns of all parties involved. This would include listening to the religious beliefs and the scientific rationale to find common ground.
- *Education and Awareness:* Efforts would be made to educate about the nature of science and technology and the core tenets of the involved religions to dispel misconceptions and foster mutual understanding.
- *Ethical Committees:* The UGC might establish ethical committees comprising religious

leaders, scientists, and ethicists to evaluate the implications of scientific and technological developments in light of religious doctrines.

- *Integration of Perspectives:* Where possible, an integration of religious and scientific perspectives would be sought, recognizing that both can offer valuable insights into the nature of existence and the universe.

- *Respect for Autonomy:* Civilizations would respect the autonomy of individuals and groups to hold religious beliefs, as long as these do not hinder the overall progress and well-being of the galaxy.

- *Compromise and Accommodation:* Where conflicts arise, the UGC would encourage compromise and accommodation, allowing for religious practices to coexist with scientific advancements, provided

they do not cause harm or impede
progress.

- *Policy Development:* The UGC
  would develop policies that
  balance the need for scientific
  advancement with the desire to
  respect and preserve religious
  traditions.
- *Conflict Resolution* Mechanisms:
  Specialized conflict resolution
  mechanisms would be in place to
  address disputes, ensuring that
  decisions are made fairly and with
  consideration of all viewpoints.

These approaches would be
underpinned by the UGC's overarching
goals of peaceful coexistence, respect for
cultural and religious diversity, and the
pursuit of knowledge and advancement
for the benefit of all civilizations within
the galaxy. The UGC would strive to
ensure that disputes are resolved in a
manner that upholds the dignity and
beliefs of all parties while also

embracing the opportunities presented by scientific and technological progress.

Can we provide an example of a specific conflict between religious beliefs and scientific advancements within the UGC?

 Here's a fictional example of a specific conflict between religious beliefs and scientific advancements within the United Galaxies Council (UGC):

In the UGC, there is a civilization known as the Zentarians. These deeply religious beings are from the planet Zentar. Their religion, Zentharism, believes that the soul is an eternal and unalterable essence that defines each individual.

The conflict arose when the Scientific Coalition of Advanced Research (SCAR), another member of the UGC, developed a technology called SoulSync. This technology claimed to be able to transfer an individual's consciousness into a synthetic body, effectively granting them immortality. SCAR intended to share this technology galaxy-wide, believing it to be the pinnacle of scientific achievement.

The Zentarians, however, viewed SoulSync as a direct violation of their religious doctrine. They believed that the soul should not be tampered with and that the natural cycle of life and death was sacred. The idea of transferring a soul, even if it were possible, was seen as an abomination.

The UGC had to navigate this delicate situation. On one hand, SoulSync represented a monumental leap in technology with the potential to eradicate death. On the other hand, it clashed with the Zentarian's core religious values.

To address the conflict, the UGC convened a special session with religious leaders, scientists, ethicists, and representatives from both SCAR and the Zentarian community. They engaged in a series of dialogues to understand the implications of SoulSync from both a scientific and religious perspective.

The outcome was a compromise. SCAR agreed to restrict the use of SoulSync technology, making it available only to those civilizations that accepted it on a voluntary basis. In turn, the Zentarians agreed to allow individual members of their civilization to choose whether to use the technology without facing ostracization.

This example illustrates how the UGC might handle a conflict where religious beliefs intersect with scientific advancements, emphasizing dialogue, respect for diverse beliefs, and searching for mutually acceptable solutions.

How did the Zentarians reconcile their religious beliefs with the new technology?

The Zentarians, facing the challenge of reconciling their religious beliefs with the new SoulSync technology, embarked on a journey of introspection and dialogue. Here's how they might have approached this reconciliation:

- *Religious Deliberation:* The Zentarian religious leaders convened councils to deeply examine the implications of SoulSync in the context of their beliefs. They sought to understand if there could be a theological interpretation that could accommodate the new technology.

- *Scientific Engagement:* Some Zentarians engaged with the scientists behind SoulSync to understand the technology thoroughly, ensuring that their religious concerns were not based on misunderstandings of the science involved.

- *Ethical Debates:* The community held widespread ethical debates, during which different viewpoints were expressed and the values of life, death, and the soul were discussed in light of the new possibilities presented by technology.
- *Individual Choice:* They recognized the importance of individual autonomy, allowing members of their civilization to make personal decisions regarding the use of SoulSync, without imposing a blanket rejection based on religious doctrine.
- *Cultural Adaptation:* The Zentarians explored ways to adapt their cultural practices to ensure that the essence of their beliefs was maintained, even if some practices were modified in

response to technological
advancements.

- *Selective Integration:* They
  considered selective integration of
  the technology, where it could be
  used in ways that did not conflict
  with core religious principles,
  such as preserving knowledge or
  for medical purposes.
- *Interfaith Dialogues:* The
  Zentarians participated in
  interfaith dialogues with other
  civilizations within the UGC to
  learn how they have handled
  similar conflicts between faith and
  technology.

Through these efforts, the Zentarians
found a balance that honored their
religious heritage while also embracing
the benefits of scientific progress. They
established guidelines for using
SoulSync that aligned with their
spiritual beliefs, ensuring that their
cultural identity remained intact as they

stepped into a new era of technological possibilities.

The Solar Systems Civilization Union (SSCU)

The Solar Systems Civilization Union (SSCU). In this reimagined story, the SSCU is a grand alliance of civilizations from within our solar system, each with its unique characteristics and home planets. Here's a creative twist on the civilizations and their corresponding planets:

- *Mercurians:* Inhabitants of Mercury, known for their speed and efficiency, adapting to the extreme temperatures of their planet.
- *Venusians:* Graceful beings from Venus, enveloped in mystery and known for their advanced atmospheric technologies.

- *Earthlings:* Humans from Earth, bringing diversity and innovation to the SSCU.
- *Martians:* A resilient civilization from Mars, experts in terraforming and sustainable habitats.
- *Jovians:* Giants from the gas giant Jupiter possess deep knowledge of energy harnessing from their planet's powerful storms.
- *Saturnians:* Ring-weavers from Saturn, skilled in creating intricate structures from the planet's rings.
- *Uranians:* Visionaries from Uranus, with a unique perspective due to their planet's sideways rotation.
- *Neptunians:* Masters of the deep from Neptune, controlling the vast oceans beneath the ice.

The SSCU is a testament to the collaborative spirit of the solar system's inhabitants, working together to ensure peace, prosperity, and progress across their celestial neighborhood. They handle disputes and share resources with the utmost respect for each civilization's cultural values and practical interests while navigating the challenges posed by their diverse environments and beliefs. The SSCU stands as a beacon of unity in the cosmos, a union where science and spirituality find harmony among the stars.

What specific environmental issues were discussed?

In our fictional narrative of the United Galaxies Council (UGC), the environmental issues that would likely be discussed are inspired by real-world concerns. Here are some specific environmental issues that could be on the UGC's agenda:

- *Climate Change:* Addressing the impact of climate change on planets and their ecosystems, focusing on reducing emissions and transitioning to renewable energy sources[1].
- *Space Debris:* Tackling the accumulation of space debris orbiting planets, which poses risks to spacecraft and satellites[1].
- *Biodiversity Loss:* Combating the loss of biodiversity due to habitat destruction, pollution, and the introduction of invasive species from interstellar travel[1].
- *Resource Depletion:* Managing the sustainable extraction and use of natural resources to prevent depletion and ensure the long-term viability of planetary environments[1].
- *Pollution:* Controlling pollution levels, including air, water, and soil pollution, which result from

industrial and technological activities[1].

- *Planetary Protection:* Establishing protocols for planetary protection to prevent contamination of celestial bodies during exploration and colonization[1].

These issues reflect a broader concern for the health and sustainability of environments across the Milky Way, mirroring the real-world urgency to address environmental degradation and climate-related security risks[23]. The UGC would work collaboratively to develop solutions that protect the diverse habitats and species within the galaxy, ensuring that all member civilizations can thrive on their home planets and beyond.

Does the UGC establish any interplanetary conservation agreements or treaties?

In the fictional universe of the United Galaxies Council (UGC), several interplanetary conservation agreements or treaties would likely be established to protect the environmental integrity of planets and their natural resources. These agreements would be similar in spirit to the real-world international environmental agreements that exist today. Here are some examples of what such treaties within the UGC might cover:

- *Intergalactic Biodiversity Treaty:* Similar to the Convention on Biological Diversity, this treaty would aim to conserve biological diversity, promote sustainable use of its components, and ensure fair sharing of benefits arising from genetic resources[1].
- *Cosmic Habitats Protection Accord:* Inspired by the Ramsar

Convention, this accord would focus on the conservation and wise use of important interplanetary habitats, ensuring their protection for future generations[1].

- *Interstellar Climate Agreement:* This would be an agreement to combat climate change on a galactic scale, setting targets for reducing greenhouse gas emissions and promoting renewable energy sources across planets[1].
- *Space Debris Management Convention:* A treaty to address the issue of space debris, outlining measures for the prevention, reduction, and safe disposal of debris to ensure the safety of space navigation[1].
- *Planetary Protection Protocol:* An agreement to prevent the cross-contamination of planets during exploration and colonization,

protecting the integrity of extraterrestrial ecosystems[1].

These fictional agreements within the UGC would reflect a collective commitment to preserving the natural heritage of the galaxy, ensuring that all member civilizations can enjoy and benefit from a healthy and sustainable cosmic environment. The principles of cooperation, scientific understanding, and respect for all forms of life would underpin them.

In our fictional narrative of the United Galaxies Council (UGC), here are the answers to your questions:

- *Earth's Reaction:* Earth, being a relatively new member of the UGC, approached the cosmic intervention with a mix of apprehension and optimism. Earth's leaders and citizens engaged in global dialogues to understand the implications of the

UGC's concerns and to collaborate on solutions.

- *Rivalries or Conflicts:* Like any large governing body, the UGC has its share of internal politics. Rivalries may arise over differing ideologies, economic interests, or historical grievances, but they are typically resolved through diplomatic channels and the UGC's conflict resolution mechanisms.
- *Dispute Resolution:* The UGC handles disputes between member civilizations through mediation, arbitration, and if necessary, a judicial system that operates on principles of fairness and intergalactic law.
- *Trade and Commerce:* Trade and commerce are vital to the UGC, facilitating the exchange of goods, services, and technologies. They play a significant role in building

interplanetary relationships and economic stability.

- *Rogue Factions:* There may be rogue factions or outliers that challenge the UGC's ideals, often driven by isolationist or extremist ideologies. The UGC addresses these challenges through diplomacy, sanctions, or, as a last resort, peacekeeping interventions.
- *Intergalactic Sports or Competitions:* Sports and competitions serve as a unifying force within the UGC, promoting camaraderie and showcasing different civilizations' physical and intellectual prowess.
- *Role of Art and Literature:* Art and literature are celebrated across the UGC for their ability to convey the depth of cultural experiences, foster empathy, and provide a common language for diverse civilizations.

- *Cultural Conflicts:* Historical cultural conflicts within the UGC have occurred, often rooted in misunderstandings or competing traditions. These are typically resolved through cultural exchange programs and education initiatives.
- *Art and Literature in Resolving Tensions:* Art and literature play a crucial role in resolving intercultural tensions by humanizing the 'other,' breaking down barriers, and opening channels for dialogue and understanding.
- *Conflicts Over Resources:* Historical conflicts over rare or unique resources have prompted the UGC to establish fair distribution systems and conservation measures to prevent such disputes.
- *Scientific Research in Resource Allocation:* Scientific research

informs resource allocation decisions within the UGC, ensuring that distribution is based on need, sustainability, and equitable access.

- *Conflicts Threatening Stability:* Historical conflicts have threatened the stability of the UGC, but they have been overcome through collective effort, shared values, and the council's strong governance structures.

- *Scientific Research in Conflict Resolution:* Scientific research aids in resolving inter-civilizational conflicts by providing objective data, fostering innovation, and offering technological solutions to underlying issues.

- *Cultural Clash Example:* A specific cultural clash within the UGC involved the Aquarians and the Solarites over the ritualistic use of a shared nebula. It was resolved by creating a schedule that respected both civilizations' practices.

- *Bridging Cultural Gaps:* Art and literature bridge cultural gaps within the UGC by sharing stories and expressions that resonate universally, promoting a deeper appreciation of each civilization's uniqueness.
- *Spiritual Practices vs. Technology:* Civilizations handle clashes between spiritual practices and technology by seeking compromises that respect religious traditions while accommodating technological progress.
- *Philosophy's Role:* Philosophy is pivotal in bridging gaps between religion and science within the UGC, offering frameworks for understanding and integrating diverse worldviews.

- *Conflicts from Technological Advancements:* Conflicts arising from technological advancements are addressed by assessing the ethical implications and societal impact, ensuring that progress benefits all.
- *Radical Groups:* There are factions that reject compromises, advocating for strict adherence to traditional values or technological supremacy. The UGC works to engage these groups in dialogue and find common ground.
- *Intergalactic Sports or Competitions:* Intergalactic sports and competitions are popular, with events like zero-gravity races and telekinetic chess tournaments drawing spectators from across the galaxy.

These responses provide a glimpse into the UGC's complex and dynamic society, highlighting the importance of cooperation, understanding, and shared goals in maintaining a peaceful and prosperous galaxy.

About the Author

Dokali (Duke) Megharief, PhD, The author of several books, including The Intellect Groups and The Prophecies Kid, The Santa of Roses, Lisa Dreams, Megharief Poetry Anthology, The Legacy and Reflections of Table 77, and three books on Business Leadership.

Disclosure:

"HARMONY ODYSSE" is a work of fiction. All characters, locations, and events are products of the author's imagination or used fictitiously. Any resemblance to actual persons, living or dead, events, or locales is purely coincidental. The names, characters, and incidents depicted are fictional and do not refer to actual individuals or entities.

The author and publisher disclaim any legal liability for any actual or perceived resemblance to real persons, living or dead, or actual events or locales. Additionally, AI was utilized to develop images and compile and linguistically edit the narrative. The stories' ideas were the creation of the author's imagination.

[225]

© 2025 Dokali Megharief
Publish: BoD · Books on Demand GmbH,
Überseering 33, 22297 Hamburg,
bod@bod.de
Print: Libri Plureos GmbH,
Friedensallee 273, 22763 Hamburg
ISBN: 978-3-8192-7945-4